STOLEN DESIRES

Curvy Girl Dark Mafia Romance

The Bratva Billionaires' Forbidden Darlings
Book 4

BARBI COX

ONE

Danya

I STAND BY THE BUFFET TABLE, EATING ANOTHER CUPCAKE, AS I ignore my lovesick brothers. Edmon is fawning over Lilah, so wrapped up in whatever she's saying, I'm sure he's going to end up stealing her before the party is over. Sienna and Lev are talking in hushed tones while avoiding others, proving that they're still tangled in the honeymoon phase of their relationship. My father and Stephanie have disappeared. I'm sure they're already at his place going at it.

Some mafia men they are. Able to ignore what we are and the politics they should play, all because they have some woman with them. I take another large bite of the cupcake as Hunter Volkov walks over.

He glances at me, then at the cupcakes. "Interesting choice, Daniel."

"A sweet tooth is safer than whatever my brothers have going on," I say after swallowing. "If I hadn't seen Lev torture someone in the last few months, I'd say he'd lost his touch."

"Words hold power. Be careful with them," Hunter advises me.

I follow his gaze to his wife. Valerie is the type of woman

a self-respecting mafia boss would want. She's strong, knows the value of silence and action, and is willing to merge into the mafia life, kill, distract, and protect even with her own life on the line.

"Your wife is one of a kind," I murmur.

"Isn't she?" Hunter grins. "No one is as vicious, smart, and sweet."

"I love my brothers, but I think they're too willing to change for the women they're interested in. Sienna is an artist who would rather ignore what Lev does. Lilah's a teacher, though she's plenty volatile when she needs to be," I say.

"And your father's woman?"

"Plenty strong in the moment. It's just the 'after' that lingers with her," I mumble. "Not that she'll be involved much. My father is determined to embrace his retirement."

"So that leaves you, alone with romance all around you," Chase says from my other side. I didn't notice him at all. He chuckles. "Don't lose your touch, Daniel."

"I have my priorities set. I know that being in the mafia isn't an obligation, it's a privilege. I get to keep my brothers safe, I get to be the family running Miami, and I don't for a second think it's a bad thing," I reply while puffing out my chest.

Valerie walks over and fits herself to Chase's side. "Boss man," she says before stretching to kiss his cheek. "There are some people who want to meet you."

"So they want to meet you, but you're being sweet?" he guesses. He puts his glass in my hand. "Whatever you think of your family, remember that we're all stronger when we have something worth fighting for."

"My family is all the incentive I need," I scoff.

Hunter shrugs at me. "Let me give you one bit of advice and I promise I won't bring anything up again."

"How can I turn that down?" I ask, because I don't want

to hear more about love when lust is so much more satisfying to fulfill.

"Coming home to someone who can love you knowing everything about you, someone who never cringes away, supports you, understands you ... it's better than hopping from one bed to another and relying on family to be there for you," he says.

He takes another cupcake, raises it to me, and heads off on his own. I roll my eyes. These cupcakes are more appealing than falling in love. Lev was right growing up, and so was Edmon–love is a weakness, just like innocence. It clouds the mind, and makes a person second guess things, and second guessing in our world means death.

As it is, we have the cartel attempting to move in–thanks to their desire for revenge on behalf of the Salinas brothers–and issues with the West Coast thanks to Gregor's inability to control himself and how my family responded. Misha's still walking around, with a few less fingers and a healthy dose of fear, but still a threat.

Since I'm the one who's available, the one who doesn't have any hangups about killing, about pausing my life to deal with what's necessary in the moment with no need to postpone, it all falls on me.

Speaking of, I check my phone. Earlier, I reached out to a few contacts to verify that everything is fine and that there's no threat on the horizon. Of course, that's not what my responses say.

Some dealers were talking about a party to hit.

Lots of action at some richy-rich venue.

Guns purchased. At least a dozen.

Fuck. I walk over to Lev and show him the messages. He nods, gripping Sienna's hand. He whispers in her ear and she touches her stomach. Sienna leans over to Lilah and they stand up, heading out the side exit.

Nodding once, Edmon walks over to me as if it's an accident. "Clearing out civilians?"

"Lev's heading outside to check things out?"

"Da," Edmon agrees as Lev does just that, playing with a cigarette between his fingers.

Edmon and I apologize to civilians, letting them know that the bride-to-be isn't feeling well. Plenty leave and for a moment, with mafia men, drunk wives, and ... well Valerie reaching under her dress for something until Lief takes her hand, shaking his head.

Perhaps it was just a few random things with no connection. I almost believe all my informants stumbled on coincidences until Lev comes back in with blood on his sleeve. He sighs. "Sienna's going to tire of me coming home shirtless. Anyone without a weapon, get to the basement and seal it off until the shooting stops."

A few people move, fewer women than plenty would think. One woman who's been throwing back liquor all night and looks like she dyes her hair gray just to enjoy the confusion sighs and pulls out two guns. She looks at another man.

"Do you have the back-up rounds?" she asks him.

I smile and pull out my Glock, eager to join in. Two seconds later, three men come in with guns, shooting. The gray-haired woman doesn't get up. She just moves to the side and takes out two of them with expert shots.

A soft yelp draws my attention, but I take out number three and notice Edmon up on the second floor. He's firing elsewhere, at different targets. Great. I cover another entrance, take out three guys, and check the guns as one pants and tries to grab my leg. "Orders."

"Yeah? Orders should be enough for me to call an ambulance for you?" I ask. I grip his arm and pull up the sleeve of his shirt.

Tattoos talk in our world and his mark says he's a low

level in the cartel. Only three kills. "How sad, dying before you fulfill your potential."

"We're far from done. You ... you'll," he chokes out.

Instead of following normal procedure and letting him bleed out or die of shock, I slide my gun into his mouth and fire. He's silent, limp, eyes open as a tear rolls over his cheek. I fire another two shots before locking and barricading the back door.

Once that's taken care of, I head back to the front with Lev. He's smoking, at ease, his face stoic. I shoot out two tires on the vehicle standing that's already got ruined windows and glance at Lev.

"Have you called the cleaners already?" I ask.

"It's only wave one. With those texts, we can expect more," he answers.

Still, no one appears out front. I glance around then, glance to the back. "Edmon was taking some hits."

"Relieve him, Danya," Lev orders.

"Yes, boss," I reply.

I head up and find Edmon tallying, finishing, and double-checking. With that, I check the back. On cue, a car pulls up. I wait, see the guns, then take two sure shots. The rest duck, start yelling, fire their automatics. Shit.

Wave one wasn't strapped like this. The gray-haired woman walks up and puts her hand out to the man beside her. "The AR-15, please."

The man pulls out an enormous gun and she sighs. "You should go inside. They're coming in the side entrances too."

"Thank you," I murmur, still amazed by her.

"Ms. Polina, they're reloading," the man says.

"No fun shooting fish in a barrel," she says.

Of course, *the* Polina. Came to get some paintings taken care of and now she's enjoying the fun–since killing for the top ranks is fun. When you move up and have someone else do the killing, I suppose a certain spark is lost until you're put back in the field.

Shrugging, I head inside. "All yours, ma'am."

I head back inside, clearing a few areas that are already packed with men eager to claim a kill. Adrenaline courses through me until I hear pounding at the door I barricaded. Snarling, I unbarricade it, then kick the door open and am hit in the face.

Another yell echoes behind me and I blink a few times, trying to clear the daze before I grab an ankle and take the guy down as he screams insults at me that only sound pretty in Spanish. I raise my bowie knife and slit his throat.

"Not interested in flirting right now. Thanks for the offer though," I huff.

I rip into three men, take one of their guns, and finish them. I wipe my face from the spray of blood there and huff. I rub my shoulder where I took a bullet. The pain won't ripple through for a while, which reminds me of the clock until emotions kick in.

Four men down right here, at least a car full taken care of out back, the first car full out front Lev can handle, Edmon ... Shit, Edmon.

I head towards him, but the door to the kitchen opens and two men appear. I shoot one in the foot and he slumps over, reaching for the wound. His head is next. The second man looks around, leaving his gut open. Messy, but simple.

Except I miss when guy three pushes his way out. Guy three is a fucking giant, too. Based on the fact he has a knife and nothing else ... I'm sure he can do more than enough damage with just that. He requires a special approach and I'm more than happy to give it to him.

I take out the guy next to him and he snorts, like its nothing at all.

Standing up, I grip my knife and my gun. He stares me down and grins. "What are you supposed to be?"

"Not much, just a name you'll never get." I set my gun down.

He grins at me and nods. "Finally, someone who understands the art of fighting."

"Art, necessity, whatever it is. You came here, and ruined a pleasant party ... so I'll make sure to ruin that face too," I say with a grin.

He comes at me with the knife, but after about three wide slashes, I wonder if all he has going for him is his size. I shove my knife into his abdomen and jerk up. Instead, he puts his blade at my throat and I hear a gun cock behind me.

Stupid me. He's a damn distraction. I shove the blade deeper and he grunts. I turn with him at the same time I hear the gunfire. But not just one, Edmon's always around.

The man in front of me gapes and digs his blade into my neck, but it's not deep enough. I'm sure of that, considering I can still breathe. He drops to the ground in front of me and I fling the knife at the guy that's still standing, even though he's gaping like a fish.

A smile turns up my lips. The man drops to the ground and Edmon waves. "I think we're clear. Ready for the cleaners?"

TWO

Abigail

I STAY WRAPPED AROUND MY FROSTED CUPCAKES, PROTECTING them as if their lives are at stake, not mine. I shudder, whimper, and then try to silence myself to stay hidden, especially when three big guys walk in.

Low conversation, then screaming, gunshots, and silence.

The silence is worse.

There's never silence in a bakery. I play music. There are people picking out sweets, kids laughing, and light conversation. Was I silly to think that catering would be the same?

When someone else walks in, I grab a frying pan and stand up, panting as my blonde hair falls into my face. I grip it with both hands, ignoring how sweaty and slippery my palms feel. When a man walks in, I swing.

He grabs it, and jerks it forward with me attached, so I fall against him. He stares down at me, his blue eyes cold, blood all over his face, something cold against my side. "Name and why you're here."

I sniff and let go of the frying pan, stepping back until I step on my cupcakes and fall over. I grab onto the counter and thank myself for postponing my diet again. My bottom cushions the fall even though my shoe is covered in frosting and cake.

The man continues to watch me, his icy, attractive face focused. He's got a little scruff, a slight bump in his nose, a cut on his neck, and blood all over him. It doesn't matter that he's gorgeous, tall, muscular, he's also homicidal, and that means saying whatever it takes to get out of here.

"Name and why you're here," he says again, pointing something at me I refuse to look at.

If I look at whatever weapon is in his hand, it will be impossible to focus on survival. "Abby! I'm Abby, the caterer."

His eyes dip down to the cupcakes. He leans his head to the side, sighs, and then sets his weapon on the table before crouching down. He takes one of the unharmed cupcakes and takes a bite, then nods once. "Sienna's choice. That's right."

I continue staring at him, not knowing what to do. He takes another bite of the cupcake and rolls out his shoulders before handing me the frying pan. "Stay here, head down, just in case. Should all be over."

"What ... what happened?" I choke out.

"Better that you don't know. You focus on these cupcakes and staying right here and I'll take care of the rest," he says, patting my head.

He rolls out his shoulder again and walks away, just like that. Since there's nothing else to do and if I think too much, I'll spiral. I clean up the ruined cupcakes, clean every single dish, then grab my coat and start taking boxes to the van. I make sure not to leave a single piece of equipment behind. Just as I finish, someone grabs me.

I jab my elbow back, turn around, and aim for the balls. The masked guy rolls on the ground, another weapon I don't want to look at, clattering at his side.

Mr. Tall, Blonde, and Bloody reappears. He nods. "There's the lookout. I told you, Ed, we missed one."

"Yeah, yeah," a repeat of the blond man says. "Hurry it up. I have a girl to get home to."

"Ah, Abby, there you are," Man 1 says with a slight smile. He looks me over and I fight the urge to cover up.

My chef shirt is a bit too small, pulled a bit too tight over my chest, and my jeans are a little too loose around my legs. Standing in front of a guy this gorgeous and lethal makes me feel like I'm more than too much. I feel too helpless too.

"Ed?" Man 1 prompts.

"Got it," man 2 says.

"Why don't you come around here? I'm curious about your cupcakes," Man 1 says, taking my limp arm and dragging me around the side of the van.

"Wh-what about them?" I ask, fighting every tremble I feel in my toes.

"I get the taste of strawberries, but the tartness of them, not the sweetness in the frosting. Nothing is too sugary or tastes fake. How do you do that?"

"I um ... it's a secret," I say, trying to focus on the conversation and not on what I just witnessed.

"Really?" He takes a step closer. "Even if I ask nicely?"

"I make my own strawberry puree using strawberries that aren't ripe. I taste everything before I add sugar and ... yeah," I say, but more tumbles out. "Plus, if you have a moist cake and you add the right amount of salt, it all balances out into something ... something good. So what just-"

"Interesting. I guess I never considered strawberries that aren't ripe," he says.

"Do you bake?"

He flashes a wide smile, made terrible by the blood on his face. "Not even a little."

"So why ... why ask?"

He just stares down at me, his smile melting me as he stares down at me. He puts one hand on my van, boxing me in. "Listen, chef, if you forget about everything that happened tonight, it'll be a lot easier. Don't ask questions about things you don't want the answer to and when Sienna inevitably asks you to make the cake for her wedding, smile, accept, and send someone else to the wedding, got it?"

I just stare at him. I don't know what else to say to him. I don't have the words. He moves closer. "Say yes."

"I don't take orders from anyone other than my clients. You're not my client," I reply.

Sighing, he shakes his head. "What's it going to take to get a yes from you? A kiss, a date, a-"

"You should take care of your shoulder and your neck. They could get infected, especially with the ... the stuff all over you," I motion to his face and neck.

Instead of looking at himself, he watches my finger as it traces my jaw and neck.

"Is that a fact? You know medical stuff, too?"

"Yeah," I say, shaking my head. "I better get back to the bakery. You, um .... you should have an easier night."

I duck under his arm and put myself in my van. I start it, then just sit there as my hands shake worse and worse. A whimper leaves my throat and my eyes water. I need to take the stuff back. I need to get the hell out of here, but I can't move. I can't see very well. I shouldn't drive, but-

"Other seat," a sharp voice says, making me yelp.

"No, I don't even know your name. You don't get to drive. You're also.. you're injured and bleeding and-"

"And holding it together a lot better than you, Cupcake. Move over or I'll move you myself," he orders, husky, deep voice, hard and unforgiving.

This isn't a man to be argued with.

I lift myself up and sit in the passenger seat. He buckles himself, shuts the door, then points at me. "Buckle."

My hands try to work but can't. He does it for me, buckling me in and patting my head again. "This GPS work?"

I nod.

Somehow, in my near-blackout haze, I miss the entire ride. I unbuckle and go to the back of the van before realizing I don't have the key. Instead, the man, whose name I still haven't gotten, twirls my keys around his fingers.

He helps me carry everything through the back doors and into the kitchen. Once that's done, I take off my apron and try to dust myself off as best I can. I let my hair down and take a slow breath. Taking off my work shirt, I sigh, feeling like I can breathe. A tank top and jeans–they're simple and easy. They're everything this situation isn't.

"Cupcake," the man says.

I turn around and find him right there, still covered in blood, yet unbothered.

"Forget about tonight. Trust me. It'll be the best for everyone. Then you won't have to deal with shit like this in the future, yeah?"

"Do you have some fancy device that will ruin my memory?" I ask.

He considers it. "I recommend a drug that will knock you out for a solid fourteen hours so you can convince yourself it was a weird dream."

I nod once, suck my bottom lip, and motion to the back door. "I'm not leaving you here unsupervised."

"You think I'll steal something?"

"I think I pay rent, I paid for everything in here, I'm the boss, and that means I'm going to stay until everyone has left," I counter, hoping I sound stronger than I feel.

Nodding, he walks out. I notice him curling into his shoulder and rubbing his neck, but I refuse to feel anything for him. He's involved in a business that I don't want to be.

I'm a baker, made the life I wanted comfortable, warm, a little tight financially, but overall what I dreamed of as a kid.

This stranger doesn't fit into it at all.

I lock up once he's outside.

I turn around, ready to give him another order, but he's gone. I glance around, shrug, then get on my Vespa. The drive home, the chilly air nipping at my nose, all of it helps relax me. Even if Florida winters are terrible, I have a cold that sinks into my bones. It's real.

Tonight *can't* be real. It has to be some kind of flu dream. I have been feeling a little off.

When I get to my little one-bedroom home, I get through a scalding shower, then stare at myself in the mirror. I'm definitely 'fully figured'. That's true. I'm short too. I pinch my hip, where there's a lot more than I want, but once I'm in my jammies, I look at myself again.

I'm cute at least. Big brown eyes, full lips, plenty in the boob and butt departments. The image of the man leaning over me, asking me how I make my strawberry frosting, flashes over my eyes. If he hadn't been covered in blood, I would have been tongue-tied. He was gorgeous, those cheek-bones, his sharp jaw, obvious muscle on him ... he should be a model.

"Nope, just a weird daydream. That's all," I say, dismissing the thoughts.

There are no bruises on me, no cuts, nothing but the normal pain in my fingers and hand from frosting so many cupcakes. Tomorrow it will all be forgotten. I'll go back to work, continue dealing with the hurt of my recent break-up, and make people smile until my smile feels easy.

So I put myself in bed, toss, turn, and stare at the clock to count how much sleep I'll get until I get a nap and my alarm goes off. Sitting up, I stretch, change into a cute floral dress, pull my hair up in a bun, and then head back to work.

"Just a normal day," I tell myself.

And it is, until right around lunch when a woman with wild red hair walks in, jerking an attractive blond guy. He has on jeans and a black turtleneck with the sleeves pushed up to his elbows, revealing tattoos along his left arm.

"Apologize," she orders.

"Sienna, I-"

"I'm sorry for last night. For both of us, all of us," she says, making me pale. "Your cupcakes and desserts were the best part and we're *both* sorry for how the night ended. You should have been escorted out before anything happened, and that's on me."

"What happened last night?" I ask, preparing a half dozen of her favorite cupcakes–the chocolate and strawberry ones. "I remember a successful catering event, nothing else."

Please don't let them notice my fingers trembling.

THREE

Danya

Good girl, I think as I stare down at the chubby little chef. Her dark gaze holds mine without flicking away. Is she fearless, repressing, or trying to prove something? There's no way she's this strong. She couldn't even leave last night. Still, the way she's looking at me, like she's preparing to throw the box at me and run bothers me.

"I appreciate that," Sienna says. "We both do. Right, Danya?"

"I'm sorry for the way things played out, but you're fine, not even a scratch, so-"

Sienna takes the cupcakes and overpays, but the baker tries to hand back the change. I shove it in her tip jar. "I'm sorry for the situation you were thrown into. I'm sorry that I scared you and that I didn't give you a choice in how shit played out."

"No clue what you're talking about. Last night was normal," she waves her hand. "Do you want anything?"

I love how she's leaning toward me, giving me a magnificent view of her cleavage. She's boiling hot. All those curves, and her determination. Very attractive.

"Nothing on the menu," I say with a smirk. "Maybe more of that excellent advice you didn't give me last night."

Her eyes dip to my shoulder, then neck. Oh, she remembers. She swallows and looks away. "I don't have more advice for you."

Is she not interested in me at all? She's not even blushing. Why do I care? I met her under less than great (for her) circumstances. I don't want her to like me, anyway. She's not my type. I like leggy, lithe blondes, tall, easy to throw around, who are only interested in a one night lay.

I lean over the counter, getting closer to her. She blinks at me, eyes going wide, full lips parting. I slide my card across the table. "If you need something along the lines of what you won't remember ... protection specifically, call me."

"That kind of thing isn't what I need help with," she mumbles, rubbing the back of her neck, not reaching for the card at all.

"Well, I owe you and I don't like owing anyone anything."

"You don't owe me anything. Like you said, not a scratch on me because nothing happened." Her smile is weaker. She leans forward. "And nothing is going to happen, right? It's not like any of what didn't happen is about me, so it's just a nightmare that I'll never have again?"

"That depends," I comment.

"On?"

"Was the whole thing a nightmare?" I ask, cocking my head to the side. "Every part? I thought some of the conversation was pretty nice, Amy."

"Abby," she corrects.

"I'm terrible with names, so how about I call you 'Cupcake'?" I ask, one side of my mouth lifting.

Her cheeks turn pink as she looks to the side and draws back. "Y-you're holding up the line."

"Trust me, they'll wait," I say, pushing my card closer to her. "This is for you alone. If someone else calls me, I'll be back and our conversation might not be so pleasant."

She takes the card and stuffs it into her shirt. Jeeze, that cleavage would distract the most dedicated hitman. Her eyes dart over my shoulder, then she sinks further back, telling someone else to man the counter. I see a guy there. He's beyond plain. Shaggy dark hair, kind of fat face compared to his thin body, but he looks ready to cause a scene.

Sienna taps her wrist, reminding me we have things to do, but I don't like the looks of this man, especially after Abby's quick exit. His eyes are on me, narrowed like he's looking for trouble, even though he'd come up to my shoulders at best.

"Something to say?" I ask.

He sizes me up and braces himself. "I'm not here to talk to you. Abigail!"

I take a menacing step closer. "It's not right to *demand* the boss of a business come talk to you. Leave. You're causing a scene."

"And you're helping," he snarls. "In fact, if you weren't here, I'd already be back there, talking to her quietly, so you're the-"

I grab his shirt and jerk him towards me, glowering down at him. "I'm what?"

"The ... the problem."

"Don't try to flip shit around. No one in here is yelling other than you. Get the fuck out," I growl.

He pushes at my hand and scurries out of the bakery. Abby must have something else going on in her life. I motion for Karik to go with Sienna, then turn and lift the stupid counter door thing and stare at a woman almost my height. She crosses her arms over her chest, hiding her name tag.

"Employees only," she blurts.

"Trust me, I'm approved," I reply.

When I try to sidestep, she steps in front of me again. "Sweetheart, I'm sure you've got plenty of other people to flirt with today. Leave Abby alone and walk away. You did a nice thing. Don't spoil it by taking credit for it."

Shrugging, I walk back out, then circle the building to the back entrance. I pull out a cigarette and put it to my lips. Two seconds later, it's snatched. "Smoking is bad for you and I don't want smoke getting into the kitchen."

Glancing down, I find Abby right there, in full 'attack mode'. It's so comparatively gentle, it's cute. I pull out another cigarette to rile her up, and she grabs the entire pack, stashing it behind her back.

"You know what I'm capable of and here you are stealing my cigarettes while hiding from some idiot half my size," I snort.

"I have my reasons," she says.

"And I have my reasons to smoke," I counter. "Who's the asshole disturbing the peace? I could have police pick him up."

"He has done nothing that would keep him in jail," she says, leaning back against the wall. "He's just ... a nuisance who doesn't want to believe we're over."

"Oh, you break his heart, Cupcake?" I ask, staring at the van from last night. No blood on it. Good. I hadn't checked it before leaving. I was riding an adrenaline high, and I was sure if I didn't leave right away, I would have jumped this girl because she was there and not sobbing. "Maybe you're more vicious than you look."

"No, I didn't," she murmurs. "He was sleeping with someone else. She texted me when she saw some shampoo I left at his place and found me in his phone. After we met up and talked. I went with her to go talk to him and he was moaning with someone else."

"Shit," I grunt.

"The other girl left, saying she wasn't dealing with it, but she was loud. He tried to tell me nothing was happening, that people were jealous, and I was just insecure. I second guessed myself until the girl came out wearing only a sheet, purring for him to come back to bed. She wasn't even upset that I was there. So I left, told him to lose my number and forget me," she answers. "Maybe not in those words. I kind of zone out when I'm upset."

I'm pretty sure I lose track of the pronouns halfway through, but I'm trying to keep up.

"And now the fuckers back, trying to convince you he did nothing wrong?" I guess.

She shrugs. "I keep avoiding him. Mona's pretty good at getting people to do what she says."

"Ah, that's why you don't need me. You already have a bodyguard," I agree, thinking of the intimidating woman who forced me to come around the back.

Abby doesn't answer and after another minute, I look over, playing with my unlit cigarette between my fingers. She scuffs her sneaker on the ground, chewing the inside of her cheek. When she meets my eyes, she looks away.

"Anyway, did you need something else? I kind of ran off," she breathes.

"You shouldn't run. Makes people feel like they have power over you."

"Yeah, well, I'm not much of a fighter, so what am I supposed to do? Confront him? Let him talk and confuse me all over again?"

"Lay down the law. If he's not buying, he has to leave. If he is buying, he takes his cupcakes and leaves, not that he deserves them. Maybe stuff a jalapeno in one and keep it until he shows up. The longer it takes, the better the revenge," I suggest.

She laughs, her entire face lighting up as her eyes crinkle

and she covers her mouth. "Maybe I'll make a wasabi frosting."

"Now you're talking," I agree with a wink. I stand up and walk over to her. "If he doesn't get off your back, call me. I have it on good authority that I'm pretty damn intimidating."

"So what, you'll be my fake boyfriend to drive away my toxic ex?" She shakes her head. "No one would believe you're into me for a second."

"Why?"

"Look at me," she says, motioning to her sexy, chubby little body. I bet I could grab her hips and slam into her without her telling me I'm being too rough. I bet her ass would look great dotted with my handprints. She nods as if I'm on the same page. "And you? No way. They'd look at us and see you doing charity or stringing things out as a joke."

I lift her chin up and study her eyes. "You forget your glasses this morning or something?"

"I don't wear glasses. I have perfect vision."

"Then your mirrors are all broken, Cupcake. Trust me, guys would ask *me* how I got *you*."

"Don't lie to me ... what's your name again?"

"Daniel."

"Danny," she whispers.

I laugh. "No, Abe. If you're going to shorten my name, do it right. Danya."

She blinks up at me, still not blushing or swooning, or anything else. "Danya?"

She says it again, more naturally, and fuck if I don't want to lean in and see how it tastes on her lips. I run my thumb over her bottom lip. "You need a fake boyfriend/bodyguard, you use that number I gave you. As long as I can be there, I will."

"Why?" she asks.

"Because Sienna's scary and she will not leave me alone

until I make up for the other night. Plus ... I'm not a fan of anyone cowering when they're in the right."

Her hand brushes mine, pushing me away. "Yeah, right. I'll call if I need something, but don't hold your breath. Based on what ..." I see a trace of fear on her face. She shakes it off and holds her head a little higher. "It seems like your talents are in short supply, so I'll only call if I need it."

"You're too damn sweet," I mumble

"Nope. Remember, I use salt and unripe strawberries," she says.

I smirk and lean closer. "I'm a bigger fan of cherry."

She takes an unsteady breath, then glances inside. "I should go."

"I'll be offended if I find out you tolerate that man again, as a heads up. Don't be stingy with my number," I advise her before walking away and lighting my cigarette.

"And I'll be offended if you smoke around me while saying you're keeping me safe," she calls.

I smile, but force it off my face as I get to the sidewalk. It's just a favor to get Sienna off my back. If I end up fake dating Abby, it might get my family to calm down about me dating, too. At no point, at *absolutely* no point, am I going to be more than sexually attracted to this girl. Period.

FOUR

Abigail

I FORGET ABOUT EVERYTHING BUT BAKING FOR THE NEXT FEW days. I have more than enough orders to keep me busy and I cling to that until Thursday when I'm doing the necessary laundry and find Daniel's card.

Daniel Ogievich. His name is a mouthful, but he's a lot of man to handle. My cheeks heat at that thought and I narrow my eyes at the card. "I mean that you're too complicated."

And here I am defending myself to a little business card. I sigh and put it in my purse. He'd be better than a Doberman if I ran into trouble. I shouldn't just brush off his offer of protection, especially when Aaron is still bothering me.

I should block his number and block him on all social media, but I don't want him showing up at the bakery again. I've worked too hard to build up my business. The last thing I need is for him to tank it with a bad Yelp review, or several bad reviews, and a bunch of yelling on a casual afternoon.

After a few deep breaths, I spoil myself with some face masks, painting my toenails, and then relaxing in a robe. I tell myself I'll make dinner, that I'll clean up my apartment, that I'll be a human, only to fall asleep ten minutes later.

I wake up to my alarm screaming and rush to get ready for work. I dig out a clean dress that's a bit more revealing than I like. It shows some thigh, reveals my shoulders, and even shows some cleavage. Oh well, I can't be choosy since my clothes didn't make it to the drier last night.

Jerking on my sneakers, I hurry downstairs to my little Vespa, throw my hair up, and rush to work. I open the bakery, pull on an apron, and get to work baking. I pride myself on making sure none of my sweets are more than a day old. Considering the morning rush, I have plenty to do, which is why I never get to wait until the sun rises to get up.

The hours pass, people come and go, and when I take my thirty-minute break with a peanut butter and jelly sandwich, I give myself all of five minutes to close my eyes. I manage two minutes (I count it), I hear my name being yelled.

Son of a biscuit, I think as I open my eyes and see Aaron approaching.

He puts his hands on his hips as he pants, his eyes focused on me. "You can read my messages but can't reply?"

"I have nothing to say to you, Aaron," I mumble.

"Come on. I messed up. Think about it, you're always working and I never get to see you. You work twelve-hour days five days a week, then work five-hour days every Saturday. I get you for *one* night and one day a week!"

"So you cheated on me and the girl you were cheating on?" I ask, trying to summon whatever strength I had while standing in front of a hitman.

"It's not like that. Molly knew we weren't serious. And the girl you saw me with, that was just a onetime thing! I have needs, okay? I'm a man. You're not taking care of them as my girlfriend, so I have to-"

"Ex-girlfriend," I correct him.

His eyes narrow in that way that always ends with his fist through a wall. "What?"

"I'm your *ex*-girlfriend."

"Don't you tell me that asshole that threw me out of your bakery is your new crush," he scoffs. "No way could you get a guy like him. You *barely* got a guy like me. It looks like you eat more than you sell and-"

"I'm perfectly healthy," I snap back. I've never tolerated anyone talking badly about my body except me. It's a stupid hill to die on, considering everything else I've tolerated from Aaron, but that's the line. "And I'm perfectly desirable."

"Uh-huh. I'll believe that he's interested in you when he says it," Aaron growls. "Until then, you're just some chick trying to get better than she deserves."

"Can I help you?" Mona growls as she opens the door.

Aaron backs down. He points at me. "I'll be back at closing."

"Great. I'll tell the police," Mona informs us. "Public harassment is great to have on a rap sheet."

Aaron flips her off but hurries away. I sigh. Mona shakes her head. "Come on. You can stand up to customers who talk down to you, and to that hot mouthy guy who came in, but not *Aaron*?"

"It's different with him," I whisper.

Mostly because something about the way he talks makes me question everything. Maybe because I've seen how angry he gets when things don't go his way. How many gaming controllers did I replace? How many holes in walls have I covered over the last year? Or the way he seems to know how things play out better than I do?

"If you don't do something, you'll never get rid of him, Abby," Mona insists. "I want you to do it for yourself, but if you can't, I will."

Mona's already done so much for me.

I distract us both with work until around five p.m. I

reach into my purse for my phone, ready to tell Aaron off via text when I feel a card prick my palm. Looking into my purse, I see Danya's card.

Sucking my bottom lip, I type in his number and send the simplest, least needy text I can come up with.

Are you available? I'm at the bakery. Closing in an hour–Abby

That's it. He'll either get it and reply or he'll ignore it and go on with his life. After all, this isn't some lethal encounter. It's not even about my pride. I know how I look next to Danya. He's a model, even if he's got blood on his face and wounds on his body. Not to mention, we're from two different worlds.

He might as well be some mafia dude from the comic I read on my phone or Death himself, like in a show I watched recently. Cold, sarcastic, uncaring about anything but whatever tally he's keeping track of.

"Do you think Aaron was serious?" Mona asks as we package up what we didn't sell today. She stares at the sign on the door. It says open to us, but to the rest of the world, we're closed. "Is he going to come back?"

"I don't know."

"I'll walk out back with you just in case," she says.

"Mona, it's not that big of a deal. He's never hurt me," I insist.

"Yeah, and I will not give him the chance to do it now," she says. "I like you. You're a good boss, and I'm not about to lose you now."

"I hate when you call me the boss. It sounds wrong."

"Yeah, yeah. You're twenty-three and your parents are all about helping with your future. I know you're a spring chicken and I'm ... five years older. It doesn't change the facts, Abby. And I'm not letting anyone hurt you," Mona says, putting her foot down.

I smile and we finish up just as my phone buzzes.

I look at it as I take off my apron and see Danya's name.

Here. Out back.

I lead Mona out back since arguing just isn't worth it and she pauses when she sees Danya leaning against our van, smoking a full ten feet from the building. His blue eyes slide over to me and he looks me over. The cigarette falls off his lip before he bites it.

My whole body feels like it's sizzling under just one long appraisal. I bite my bottom lip and try to ignore the goose-bumps along my arms and legs as I walk toward him.

Mona nods. "Good choice. Good night."

She turns to go her own way, leaving me alone with Danya in the low yellow light from the one streetlight back here. Danya turns to face me, his shoulder still on my van. "You used my number."

"You encouraged me to," I say defensively.

"What is it, Cupcake? Need someone to sample some new flavors?" his eyes dip down to my chest. "Something off the menu?"

Is he flirting with me? No. It has to be sarcasm. I clear my throat. "My ex is making himself a bigger problem. He said he was going to be here and ..."

"And brought up our interaction the other day?" he snorts.

"Maybe. You didn't tell me you threw him out," I murmur.

"He was a bit too heavy for me to toss. I went to the gym that day though. I've been bulking up so I can toss him the right way," Danya answers. "So, a fake boyfriend gig?"

"It's not my go-to. I will not ask you to lie or anything. If you wouldn't mind just ... coming around the shop a few times a week. I'll send you home with free cupcakes. Sienna likes them," I say, trying to sweeten the deal. "She can't be mad if you're giving her the sweets she loves."

"I might just need the frosting after a bit," he says before exhaling away from me.

Why does that sound so dirty coming from him? I nibble my lip and he smirks before leaning closer to me. "Your mind's in the gutter. How about you tell me what's going on in your head, Cupcake?"

"Nothing!" I blurt.

He chuckles, then backs me against the van. His cigarette is close to my face. I almost cover my nose, but he drops the cigarette and steps on it without looking away from me. "You don't want me to lie for you?"

"No. I don't like lying."

"You're damn good at it, pretending that nothing happened the night we met."

"Danya," I say in a breathy voice. "That was just a nightmare."

"Then what's this?" he asks while coaxing my chin up with a finger. "Because I'm *going* to lie."

"What?" I breathe.

"I'm going to tell that asshole and any other fucker who wants to try their luck with you that you're mine," he says, leaning down until my nose brushes his. "And you're going to be a good girl for me and agree, aren't you?"

I shudder and realize I'm holding onto his shirt, even though I don't remember deciding to do that. I nod slowly. "I will."

He grins and kisses the corner of my mouth. "You're so good at acting for me, Abe. Boyfriend wannabe is watching us. No, no," he murmurs, so I can feel his words on my lips. "Don't look. You're mine right now, remember?"

"I'll say we're together then, but I don't know who will believe me," I answer.

"There are ways to convince them," he answers, turning my chin to the side and running his lips over my neck. "We'll only act when it comes to words."

When he bites my throat, then licks across my skin, I squeak. "What ... what do you call this?"

"This is a direct result of that damn dress you have on." He kisses further down my neck, then bites my shoulder harder, making me hiss. One of his arms wraps around my waist, jerking me against him as he continues to lick, suck, bite.

I should push him away. This is too much. I'm not this kind of girl. Then again, I'm not the best at saying 'no' either. I hate confrontation. And do I want to push him away when his hot mouth feels so good? When his muscled body against mine is better than just about anything I've ever fantasized about?

"And that is because I was right," he says when he draws back.

I stare up at him, dizzy. "About what?"

"You taste even better than your desserts," he says, a cocky smile turning up the corner of his lips.

FIVE

Danya
_____

I never said I wouldn't *enjoy* being her fake boyfriend. Seems like the best way to have a relationship, honestly. Excuses to kiss her, tease her, touch her, without the commitment of actually being together. Based on the gaze I can feel trying to burn a hole in the back of my head, I know her ex-boyfriend is pissed too.

That means I'm winning all around.

"Danya," Abby says breathlessly. "Um, we ... if it's fake, then.."

"We're selling it. That hickey on you will do plenty. Now, I'm going to take you home because I don't trust that little *almost* motorcycle you have."

"She's dependable!" Abby argues.

I chuckle. "I think I just proved I am, too. Do I need to put you over my shoulder and carry you to my car?"

"Don't you dare. My feet belong on the ground," she insists.

I almost tease her about her sex life, but I notice the way she touches her little belly. And compared to her tits and hips, her belly *is* little. She just doesn't see it the right way. Maybe I can fix that.

"Hold my hand and pretend you like me," I order her.

She obeys, taking my hand as she looks up at me again. "I'm jealous of your eyelashes. They're pretty."

I scoff. "That's what you're going to compliment?"

"Am I supposed to compliment your butt? I didn't get to see it today," she muses, thinking out loud.

Rolling my eyes, I lead her to the main road. "You need more lights back here."

"Danya," she says.

"I'm serious. Bad people see dark places and treat it like an opportunity," I say. When we get to the road, I notice the ex standing there. I motion to him. "See?"

"What are you doing with my girlfriend?" The asshole demands.

I look at him. "Do I know you? Your annoying voice rings a bell."

"Aaron, you should go," Abby says, her voice all demure and quiet.

"You're more prickly with me than him and you like me," I point out to her.

She blushes and squeezes my hand. He either scares her, or something else is going on. I'm offended. I'm not as scary as he is in her eyes. She should consider glasses.

"Yeah ... well ..." she trails off, then shrugs.

I sigh. "Whatever your name is, get out of here. I'm not interested in being late for our reservations."

He narrows his eyes at me. "I know this isn't real. There's no way you'd date her."

"You mean Cupcake here?" I ask, motioning to Abby.

"Dude, it's obvious. You're in some kind of slump or something. Abby, he's just going to dump you or cheat on you," the guy insists. "One leggy blonde and he's gone."

Well, he wouldn't be wrong, but I did my research on Abigail. "Abigail is a successful business owner, graduated culinary school a year early, manages all her shit herself, can handle stress like a pro, and is sexy as hell on top of it. Where am I going to find better?"

Both of them stare at me. I cup Abby's cheek and lean down, licking across her bottom lip and making sure her ex sees it. I grin. "Plus, you taste like frosting."

I'm pretty sure her red cheeks are lighting the entire walkway by the time I pull away. I glower at the asshole kid standing in our way. "You lost her. Give it up and don't get in my fucking way."

He swallows hard and backs up. Weasels always recognize when there's a bigger predator playing. He scuttles back and mumbles something, but I guide Abby to my car. I open the door for her and lean in to buckle her.

She swats at my hands. "I can buckle myself!"

"So independent. You're cute," I pinch her cheek.

Abby begrudgingly guides me to her apartment and keeps telling me I don't have to come up. I don't bother to answer. I just keep following. She struggles with the lock twice, then opens it. She doesn't let me in.

"Give me a minute to tidy up," she says.

"I don't care about a mess." I jiggle her door knob. "This is a problem, though. It's loose."

She gives me tools and I'm so focused on the doorknob that when I finish up after testing it; I realize she's a little flushed and her place looks overall clean. She's sentimental, though. She has pictures everywhere, little paintings that must have been done by a friend, and other things around her apartment.

"I don't get a lot of time to do housekeeping or ... cooking ... or anything," she sighs before collapsing on her couch.

"Pizza it is," I decide.

I hand her my phone so she can order, then shrug, order the pizza, and look over at her. "What should I know about you since we're dating?"

She blinks at me. "Um ... I work a lot. Probably too much. I'm a perfectionist. I don't trust work done by anyone but me. I studied medicine for a bit, but I can't do needles, so washed out. I don't go out to party or anything. I don't have many friends. Mona's probably the closest thing I have to a friend, but she just sees me as a boss. My parents live in Boca. Dad's a successful lawyer. Mom's a hairstylist. I've never been out of the country, but I have seen the Grand Canyon."

I nod once.

"Anything else?"

"I'm *not* a fan of PDA," she says, shooting a glare at me. "Especially not when it's making someone else jealous."

"Our whole relationship is to make him jealous then leave, Cupcake," I say.

She touches her bottom lip. "I think some rules are more important."

"Wow, you don't want to know me, want to put in a bunch of rules. You're a demanding little thing," I snort.

"I'm serious, Danya," she insists. "I know this is fake. You know this is fake. Aaron *shouldn't* know it's fake because I'll look twice as pathetic for buying you off with cupcakes. I want to have some things straight."

I consider that, but she rubs her shoulder for a moment. "What should I know about you?"

"I'm lethal and scary. I hate sweets, but like your cupcakes, which is why I asked about them when we met. My brother is more terrible than I am but hides it better. I'm not interested in relationships or anything long-term. I'm a workaholic and you shouldn't ever ask about what I do. Other than that, I like tattoos—I consider that self-care—and I know how to piss exes off. Also, I hate rules ... and authority ... and laws since they never take into account what's necessary."

She blinks at me for a long moment. "So that's why you don't want rules."

"That's what you're taking from my very nice speech?"

"How can you handle tattoos? It's hours of being stabbed," she says, still not reacting the way I plan for her to.

"Abigail, you're ignoring the giant elephant in what I just told you," I point out.

"I know you're in the mafia, Danya. It's shockingly obvious. I mean, come on, I cater a family event and they attacked you guys. You and your twin take people out like its nothing. Sienna wasn't surprised. A single hitman wouldn't include his family. I saw you covered in blood. And I know you like my cupcakes," she says, holding herself a little taller.

I shake my head ever so slightly, despite my smile. "You're something, Abe."

"But tattoos are relaxing to you?"

"It's a controlled pain. Trust me, I've had worse. Plus, I like having artwork on my body. I'm a gallery–and I don't just mean my good looks," I say with a wink.

She rolls her eyes. "So, the rules–with the reasons so they work for you."

I groan.

"No kissing unless it's necessary. Otherwise, it's not pretend–pretty simple," she says, then narrows her eyes at me. "Definitely no sex. There's no reason for us to go there, and I believe it's a loving thing."

"Prude."

"I am not!" she says, but her cheeks turn bright red. "I just ... I've only been with two people and I was dating both of them and waited until I knew I meant something to them and they meant something to me ... or that's what I thought, anyway."

"Okay, limited kissing, no sex. What else?"

"If you go out with someone else, I don't care. Just don't let Aaron see you. And this doesn't have to last longer than like two weeks. He'll forget all about me by then," she says.

"Are you allergic to anything?" I ask.

"Um ... yeah. I'm allergic to lobster and penicillin," she mumbles. "Lobster is a death-level allergy, so don't even come close to kissing me if you've eaten it. Penicillin will just make me gross."

"Got it."

"You?"

"Bullets," I mumble.

She rolls her eyes. "Everyone's allergic to bullets."

We go back and forth about more of the basics until the pizza arrives. As we eat, I find out she has some very intense opinions. She hates bowling because she refuses to trust that the employees are paid enough to clean the shoes every single day. And she has a thing against hot fruit–on pie, no pineapple on pizza, and no pineapple upside-down cake. She also hates leggings with a passion that borders on insanity.

When I choke on my pizza, laughing at her, she shoves me. "You're so mean!"

"And you're mean right back. Like an angry little squirrel. It's cute," I tease.

She slugs my shoulder.

I remember then that she took down a member of the cartel without even looking. She hadn't been shy then. Of course, she'd looked like she was ready to apologize, but Abby's more than her ex thinks she is. I'm pretty sure she's more than *she* thinks she is, too.

After we finish the pizza, she stands and stretches. I groan as more of her body shows under the dress. When the hem rises to show her ass, I can feel myself getting hard.

Damn, this is going to be a very hard two weeks. I can already feel the blue balls setting in.

Abby leads me to the door and sighs. "I need to get to sleep."

"It's not even eight p.m.," I point out.

"And I get up at four a.m.," she says with a shrug. "Be a good fake boyfriend and support my sleep schedule."

"I'd rather ruin it," I flirt, resting my arm on the door frame as I lean toward her. "I'm also not convinced you can sell a kiss you enjoy, Cupcake."

"I just purse my lips and-"

As she starts to demonstrate, I roll my eyes and cover her mouth. "I'm starting to believe you're a virgin and you've never been kissed properly."

She narrows her eyes at me. I notice the hickey I left on her and free her mouth just to stroke it. "At least you've now had a hickey. We'll work on the rest."

"Danya, this is fake," she says for the tenth time.

"I'm well aware of my title. Fake boyfriend, here for you to toss around as you need. I'll see if ex-boyfriend is going out anytime soon. If he sees us together being natural, he'll buy this a lot more."

"Fine. But that only works on Saturdays," she says. "It's the only night I can be out until around ten or eleven."

"Sure thing, Cupcake. I'll see you Saturday, unless you miss me tomorrow afternoon," I hint.

"Saturday it is," she says, before pushing me away and shutting the door.

Sweet, yet sharp. I like Abby already.

SIX

Abigail

I SPEND ALL OF FRIDAY TRYING TO CALM DOWN AFTER BEING around Danya. I have no illusion that he'll forget we're in a fake relationship. I do have doubts about my ability to walk away when the time comes. That's the real reason behind the rules. If we don't kiss unless we have to, I can't forget that he's not mine. If we don't have sex, I can't get attached. It should be that easy.

Even if I enjoy being around him and I like how he lets me be sassy, how he welcomes it and always makes it fun. Even if I like looking at him, even if I've never felt hotter, more attractive, or more turned on than when he was kissing my neck and talking dirty to me right there in a parking lot ... he's not mine.

No commitments. I'm betting it's because he's in the mafia. I get it. It's not just work, it's his life. Maybe I'm not in a good place for a relationship either. I just ended things with a guy I'd been with for a year. I work crazy hours. I'm rarely available and I don't want to change that, since that means trusting someone else in my kitchen. And what the hell am I thinking? He's in the mafia!

Saturday at work, though, I consider how nice it would

be to have someone else in the kitchen. I've written all my recipes in case someone needs to take over for me at some point. Maybe if I took two days off a week, I'd be able to create more recipes or see my parents more, and see my friends when they ask me to go out and be a person, not just a kitchen appliance.

Then again, what if it goes wrong? What if I miss out on an opportunity because I'm not here? Whatever, that choice can wait.

Eli, the guy who works with me on weekends, sings off-key as we work in the kitchen. He flashes a flirtatious smile. He's nineteen. Seems like they keep getting younger and more aggressive.

"So, Miss Abby, it's been pretty slow today. What if we closed up early and you teach me how to make frosting?"

"You know, our biggest rush is around four. Mona will be in soon and that means-"

"I know, I know," he huffs.

He tried flirting with her *once*. Mona doesn't allow second chances, that's for sure. When she comes in, I'm worried about taking two cupcakes, but she forces me to and then kicks me out of the shop.

I head home, take a quick nap, then text Danya, trying to figure out what we're doing. He just tells me to look sexy. Groaning, I clean myself up, making myself as perfect as possible. I leave my hair down and wiggle into a pink dress. It's a little tighter than I remember, and a little shorter, but the skirt isn't clinging to my hips, so I consider it a win. Even if the sleeves keep falling down my shoulders.

I slide into flats just as I hear a knock at my door. I open it and look up at Danya. He inspects my face, running his thumb under my bottom lip. "You have pouty lips. Are you teasing me?"

"I have cupcakes for you," I say instead, pulling away from his hand and showing him the box. "You can bring them to Sienna. They're her real favorite — cookies and cream."

He sighs. "So professional."

"And proud of it. Where are we going?"

"To a lounge. It's not a club, I promise, but it's not just a bar. There's food and dancing and shit. Aaron is taking a date there tonight. Seeing you will fuck with him plenty," Danya promises me.

"Are you really available on Saturday nights?"

"Yeah. Police presence is always higher on Fridays and Saturdays. It's better for me to work on weekdays," he says as if it's nothing.

I realize then he's in slacks and a black button-up. He pushed the sleeves up past his elbows and he keeps fumbling with the top two buttons. I take his hand. "Why are you so uncomfortable?"

"This place has a dress code. I'm not fond of fancy clothes," he huffs.

"We'll have dinner and leave," I say, then drag him downstairs.

I don't let him hold the door for me and he speeds like a maniac through the city. Every yellow light must mean 'step on it' because that's what he does. When we arrive, I'm breathless and sure that I've left nail marks on the car door's little armrest.

"From now on, I drive," I say.

He shakes his head. "Criticizing my driving already? What is this, our two-month anniversary?"

Danya keeps his smile as he wraps his arm around my hip and pulls me close. "I can't have you getting cold."

Just like that, my cheeks set ablaze. We get a few looks as we walk in, but I'm pretty sure everyone's focused on how tall and good looking Danya is. I barely come up to his shoulder, so I'm not surprised that I'm overlooked.

Once we're seated, Danya orders vodka for us. I almost

laugh when he says to add a splash of cranberry to our drinks. His eyes flick around the room and his lips curl. "This *will be* a quick night."

"Problem?"

"We're on the edge of my territory. I don't want you ruffled if a fight breaks out."

"Great. I should have rethought you as my fake boyfriend," I grumble as I look over the menu.

"Make me pay for it. Order everything except the lobster."

I blink a few times, then peek at him over my menu. Did he remember that I'm allergic? We order food and he gets steak. I decide to get a salad until Danya stares at me like I'm insulting him. I switch to the chicken Alfredo.

"Salads are a starter, not a meal," he says. "Take my hand."

I obey, trying to ignore how good his fingers feel in mine. His hand is so big and warm. Danya looks at my fingers and grins. "You have cute fingers. You dislocated the middle one once, didn't you?"

"I ... I did," I agree.

"It's bent more than the others. You didn't go to the doctor."

"I put it back in place myself," I mumble.

"You know, I don't get this, Abby. You're strong as hell. You took out a dude, came at me with a frying pan, and you're afraid of some pitiful asshole?"

"It's different with him," I answer, while pulling my hand away. Danya tightens his hold on me instead. "With you, I don't get ... confused. I can and will defend myself physically, but I don't trust myself with Aaron. It's like ... I don't know, like my head gets all weird and foggy and I can't be sure what's real."

"You're giving him too much power. You own a business. Create your own recipes. You trust yourself plenty. If anything, you should be angry. He cheated on you! The girl he cheated with had more balls than he did."

"Yeah, yeah," I grumble. "I don't want to talk about this."

"Sure."

We eat while talking about the weather–literally–and going through every 'small talk' piece and icebreaker we know. It's awkward. When we finish eating, Danya stands. "Let's dance."

"I don't dance."

"Oh, you're about to. I can and will pick you up," he threatens me. "Do you want a scene or-"

"Fine!"

Danya leads me to the dance floor and pulls me close. We just kind of sway until he spins me under his arm, twirls me out until our arms are stretched, then draws me back to him with a smile. I shake my head. "I'd never guess you can dance."

"Of course. I have to be elite in everything. I'm a perfectionist," he says.

We keep dancing until someone bumps me. I look over and see Aaron with some pretty brunette. She's thinner than me, with a delicate smile I wish I had. She apologizes, but Aaron just glares.

Danya pulls me back to him and rests his hand lower on my back, his pinky grazing the curve of my ass. I suck in a breath and look up at him as he draws me tighter against his body. "Ignore him."

"Danya-"

"Cupcake, ignore him. I'm serious. You won't grow if you keep looking back," he says. "Plus, if you keep giving him attention, I'll want to shoot him."

"You don't have a gun," I whisper.

Danya comes to a dead stop and jerks me against him. I feel something hard against my hip and look down. Danya leans down to whisper in my ear. "That's not my cock poking you, Abigail. My cock's a lot bigger."

I shudder and draw back to stare up at him. "I ... um ..."

He spins me around so I can process that information. When the song ends, Danya insists we pay, then leads me outside as we wait for the valet. I clear my throat. "You carry that with you?"

"All the time. I feel naked without one."

"So beach dates?"

"Not a thing as far as I'm concerned," he answers, glancing around. "Come here, please."

I hug him and rub his sides. He cups the back of my head. "If the wrong people see you, you *will* become a target."

"We shouldn't have come here."

"I don't mind. I might charge you more than cupcakes if I have to kill someone, though, Abby," he warns me. "Fuck. I'm so tired of shitty timing."

I lift my head and find him staring at me. "It's a need."

"It?"

He lifts my chin and leans down. "Not just a need though, Cupcake. After licking your lip, I wanted to taste a lot more."

That's all the warning I get. Danya kisses me and everything slows down, his lips pressing to mine, molding, but he does nothing halfway. He sucks my bottom lip, nibbles my top lip, then licks between my lips. I hesitate.

I don't like PDA. I said that. But he said it's a need. Do we need to do more than this? His lips open against mine and I can't calm my curiosity. What does a hitman taste like? His hand tightens in my hair as his tongue teases mine with long, slow strokes that make me feel hot and gooey.

Tightening my hold on his shirt, I press my body closer to his. He changes the angle ever so slightly and kisses me faster, deeper. Everything is more, feeding the steadily growing fire in my belly.

His hand tightens in my dress and a low moan echoes between us. I don't know if it's me or Danya, but I'm suddenly *very* okay with kissing him. He nips my bottom lip, then renews the kiss again, taking control, so all I can do is swoon as I try to keep some kind of control.

My legs shake and all I can think about is how he'd kiss me if he liked me, if he wanted me. If this is fake ...

A throat clears and Danya pulls away before placing one soft, chaste kiss on my lips. I pant, trying to cool my cheeks. Well ... no one's ever kissed me like that, like they wanted to taste every secret I've ever kept and know just how to learn everything without asking me a single question.

"Your car, sir," the valet says.

"Ah, thank you," Danya says before tipping him. He leads me to his car, opens the door, and kisses me again. His eyes burn through me until I'm so sure that I'm wet, I'm embarrassed. "The next time I come to the bakery, I'm not accepting cupcakes."

"What?"

He winks at me and shuts the door. I stare out the windshield and see Aaron standing there, his teeth clenched, cheeks red, his hands curled into fists at his sides.

It was just acting, I remind myself despite touching my lip and wondering if it's wrong to put us in situations where Danya *has* to kiss me.

SEVEN

Danya

EVEN AFTER DROPPING ABBY OFF, I CAN STILL TASTE HER. I touch my lips, expecting to still feel her lip gloss or whatever there. Shaking my head, I step on the gas. Not only had her ex walked out, but I'd seen Misha. That asshole was talking with the cartel. The thought of that alone pisses me off. I want to turn around and take them out right now.

Why wait for my brother's approval? He'll approve after the fact. I glance in the passenger seat as I wait at a red light. I see the box of cupcakes that I need to deliver to Sienna, then I can talk to Lev or Vasily or whatever he wants to call himself today.

I arrive at the mansion and bang on the door until Karik opens the door. I sigh. "Are they fucking again?"

"Is that you, Edmon?" Sienna asks.

"No, why is Ed coming over?" I ask. "Is he having more problems with Lilah?"

"No, talk about Misha. Misha's made more threats to your dad, I guess."

"Things you're not supposed to know," Lev says as he kisses the top of Sienna's head.

43

She rolls her eyes. "I can handle threats. That's how we got together."

I offer her the box of cupcakes. She looks at them, then narrows her eyes at me. "Did you hold that poor baker hostage for cupcakes?"

"No. I'm doing her a favor and she suggested giving you cupcakes," I say.

During the meeting with Ed–once he shows up, with fresh hickeys on his neck–Lev, and our father, I can't stop thinking about the threat to Abby. It's not that I care about her, but she's innocent. A civilian trying to put her life back together after a breakup. She doesn't deserve more stress. When I mention seeing Misha with some cartel guys, the room goes silent.

"Where were you?" Vasily asks.

"Lugosi's," I answer. "On the border. I covered myself, so they didn't see me," I say, giving only the information they need, nothing else.

"They're moving in closer," our father says. "I don't like this. They're testing the waters."

"Misha needs to lose more than his fingers," Vasily agrees. "Ed?"

"Can do."

"Danya, back him up. Make sure Misha's off the map," Vasily says as his fingers interlock and release again and again. Before Ed and I get to the door, he has us stop. "Figure out what he's saying first."

"You want us to bug him?" I groan. "We have to wait?"

"It's better to make sure we're taking out the right people," Vasily says.

"Misha is the right person to take out. He'll be leaking information if we don't do something," I argue.

The room is silent. Vasily stands, both hands on the desk. "We thought that when our father took out Gregor. Now look at this."

"This is our life!" Edmon disagrees. "There will always be people who want us dead. That is our existence."

Which is reason enough to fake out the rest of this time with Abby and be done with her. I pinch the bridge of my nose. I take a few deep breaths. "Fine, we'll bug his house and car and then we'll act. Only because you're the boss. That's the only reason I'm not cornering and killing him."

Vasily tries to say something, but I walk out to my car and light a cigarette. Edmon walks out and stands near me. "You like being careful. What's going on?"

"Every time we've hesitated since Sienna came back into our lives, it's ended in disaster. There are shootouts, there are threats to us. The Volkovs took on every threat, they attacked head on and they own D.C. No one dares to challenge them."

"They don't have to deal with cartels like we do," Ed argues. "It has nothing to do with Lev getting married."

"Vasily," I remind him.

"It's Lev in the mafia. Let Sienna call him whatever she wants. He's still Lev. What is the real issue?" Ed demands.

I exhale smoke, then crush the cigarette between my fingers. I'm too frustrated to be patient enough for the nicotine to work. I take a slow breath. "I'm fake dating the baker. I owed her after the whole ... her seeing the cartel rush into the party thing. Sienna dragged me in to apologize one day and I'm following through."

Ed cocks his head to the side. "That hard to get dates?"

I flip him off. "It's two weeks, but I don't want some civilian getting stuck in the crossfire, especially knowing Sienna will turn *Lev* on me if I take away the woman she wants to make the wedding cake."

"That's true. She will kick your ass. She might do worse if Lev gives her a gun," Ed chuckles.

I roll my eyes. "I'm also fucking tired, man. That siege had things getting ... uncomfortably real. I love a fight as much as you do, but having a knife digging into my throat and a bullet through my shoulder was a little too close."

Ed nods. "Yeah. It wasn't great."

"I just want it done so we can enjoy a little more peace, you know? I can't even get off when all this action is going on."

"Liar."

"Fine, I can jerk off whenever, but I'd like a vacation for a bit," I huff.

He rolls his eyes.

I take myself home, to an apartment because I'm saving up for my eventual retirement, but after working out for thirty minutes, I know sleep isn't going to come easily tonight. I'm not worried about Abby, not yet, but I don't want to get to that point.

When I get through a shower and put myself in bed, I think about her again. The needy way she kissed me, how her body pressed to mine, how damn good she tasted. I was tempted to grab her ass, wanted to do a lot more than make out while waiting for my car, but didn't.

Because I'm damn respectful of her rules. They have reasons behind them. Not that my cock cares, considering it's hard when she's around.

Sleep isn't going to come with this tenting my sheets. Sighing, I squirt some warming lube into my hand, then close my eyes and stroke myself while thinking about Abby. In that damn pink dress. It was so tight around her tits, so short, showing off her thick thighs. It would have been so easy to slide my fingers up her legs in the car, to pull over, put her on the hood, and fuck her.

She wouldn't complain about me breaking rules after I ripped the front of her dress and showed her how good my mouth would feel all over her body, how much she'd like my fingers inside her, my cock filling her sweet pussy.

Groaning, I thrust my hips into my hand, tightening my

fingers around myself as I imagine her wet pussy squeezing around me. She'd moan for me, just like she did while kissing me. I can imagine her panting and whimpering like when I kissed over her neck, her perfect plush body pressed to mine, for me to lick, taste, touch, fuck

My toes curl and I grip my pillow with one hand as my hips lift off the bed. I finish into my palm and shudder. Naked, in my bed, the sheet barely covering me, and I've finished in record time. All thanks to the baker who refuses to explore the possibilities with me. Her and those damn rules.

She's going to eat her words. I'll prove I'm more than some angry asshole who's willing to make her ex jealous. I'll prove that her ex isn't who she should be with. She should give a man like me a shot. Someone who can worship her and build her up all at the same time. The kind of man who won't cheat on her, who will kill for her, who will burn down everything but her bakery and her little apartment if it means keeping her safe and happy.

That's the wholesome, happy thought that helps me drift off to sleep.

———

Monday, after a long workout session and cleaning every gun and weapon I own, I head to the bakery. Considering Aaron the Asshole saw Abby and me over the weekend, I'm anticipating him causing a scene.

I'm not disappointed either. He's in the store, yelling over the counter. Luckily, there's only one other person in the shop and the woman is looking at Aaron like he's a disappointment to the entire species.

I walk in, dinging the bell, but he doesn't turn around. So I just stand behind him.

"If you would have kissed me like that more often, maybe we'd still be together! Maybe I would have felt loved!" Aaron yells. "But, let's be honest, the other dude started it because that's what you need. You never start anything yourself when it comes to physical stuff. You're married to your damn pastries!"

"That's enough," Abby says, her voice stronger than I remember, but still soft. "This is a public space and you are disturbing the peace and ..."

Her eyes shift, meeting mine, and I smirk at her as she blushes. She cleans the counter.

"And what? Did you run out of words?" Aaron demands. "You don't have anything to say to me, do you? I bet you were just with me because I agreed."

I walk around Aaron and lean on the counter. "Hi, cupcake."

She blushes deeper. "Danya."

"Do better," I murmur before raising my voice so Aaron hears. "How was work this weekend? We didn't have much time to talk about it Sunday morning."

Her lips part. "Don't say that in public!"

I chuckle. It's so much fun ruffling her feathers. A few lies will sell our relationship. "You're so damn cute. I love that you play hard to get, you know? Salty and sweet at the same time."

"Keep this up and I'll .... I'll-"

"Play fight with me again? I liked the wrestling part. You've got a hell of a right hook, though. You'll have to be careful or you're going to hurt spots on me I know you like," I purr.

"You're interrupting," a voice from behind me says.

I wave my hand. "Yeah, I'm so sorry that your bitching has to wait. How about you save yourself the energy," I say, refocusing on Abby. "So, cupcake, can I buy you dinner tonight? I promise I'll leave by eight. I'll even tuck you in."

"No!" she gasps. "If you do that ..."

"I know, I know, we'll be up too late," I sigh as if we've

lived that kind of night before. "You sleep better once you're satisfied, though."

"You asshole, this is a public place!" Aaron yells behind me.

"One second, Abby," I mumble. I turn around and look over at Aaron. "Oh, just you. If you want to yell at something a little closer to your level, there's a dumpster out back."

His fists shake.

I arch an eyebrow at his silence. "I could show you the way. It's easy to miss, just like you."

"You-you-you.."

"I know. I tie tongues all the time. I'm less interested in yours, though. Shoo," I motion for him to leave. "The adults are talking. If you're not done with your temper tantrum, I can call your babysitter."

He throws a punch and I catch it without a problem. I jerk him closer to me so I can whisper in his ear. "Show up here again and I'll break your hand. Since my girlfriend is watching, I'm being nice. If you don't want a hefty hospital bill, fucking scram."

"You can't-"

I pop one finger out of place, making him grunt, then draw back so he knows I'm serious. "Scram or scream."

EIGHT

Abigail

I WATCH AARON SCUTTLE FROM THE BAKERY WITHOUT looking back once. I glance at Mona and she motions for me to go. I gape. "We still have-"

"More than enough pastries for today. You're the boss, and your sexy hunk of a new boyfriend is here. Go," she insists, keeping her voice down.

"I told you that it's all-" I hiss.

"Shut up. Fake never means fake. You can't fake a blush. Go," she orders me.

Sighing, I hang up my apron and walk around the counter. I take Danya's hand and lead him out of the shop. He pulls out a cigarette that I take. He narrows his eyes. "You won't like me on withdrawals."

"Try the patch or something," I say.

He looks me over, then twirls a lock of my hair around his fingers. "I could be bribed."

"Danya-"

"We both liked that kiss."

"It was fake."

"I said I'd lie with words, not with actions," he croons, grabbing my shirt and pulling me toward him. His nose brushes mine and I take an unsteady breath. "Are you going to lie to me and say you didn't like it too?"

"You're intense."

"I am. Answer the question."

"You didn't ask one," I counter. "You demand things."

He chuckles. "Did you like kissing me?"

"At the moment, yes, but it opened a lot of questions," I answer before lifting my eyes to his. "We have rules."

"Very annoying rules right now."

"Lucky you, I just got forced out of my bakery. I owe you dinner. Maybe I can cook for you ... if I remember how."

"Or I'll cook and you'll owe me double," he says.

"Danya!" I try to argue.

He still gets me into my car and to my apartment without listening to even one of my reasonable arguments. We both stand in front of my door. Danya arches an eyebrow. "What?"

"I never said you could come in."

"You offered to cook. That's an invitation, Abe," he says. "Do I have to search you for your keys?"

His eyes darken as he looks me over and his lips part ever so slightly. I swallow hard as my face heats. I touch my cheek. Why can't I control my body around him? I've never blushed like this around anyone. Maybe he's got some kind of magic spell over me or something. Maybe it's that damn kiss or the fact that I know he could kill me, but he's always gentle with me instead.

"Tick-Tock," he says, a lot closer. "If you don't turn over the key, I'm going to give you a very thorough search right here in the doorway."

I fish my keys out of my pocket and shakily put it in the door, getting it open on the first try and jerking Danya in. I slam the door shut and try to calm my heart. Danya rests his forearm by my head, leaning toward me.

"You're all worked up today, aren't you?" he asks. He studies my face before I can answer. "What did the ex say before I came in?"

"I don't know. It was loud, mean ... more of the same," I answer.

He sighs and pushes off the door - even though I kind of expected him to kiss me - and goes right to the kitchen. I try to stop him, but he turns, lifts me onto the counter, and sets me there. I'm higher than I ever want to be, but I don't trust my ability to hop down without tripping and causing a whole commotion.

Danya works on pulling things out and looking through my fridge, freezer, and pantry until he has enough to make a meal. He hums to himself as he works, then turns to me and rubs my knee.

"Abby ..."

"Please don't give me more advice. I don't need it," I whisper.

"I know you don't need my advice," he breathes. "I just don't want you to belittle yourself because of some asshole that never deserved you."

"You say that like you *deserve* me!" I say, nearly yelling before I swallow.

Danya walks over and slides his hand around the back of my neck. He glances at my lips, then steadies his gaze on my eyes. "I don't deserve you, cupcake. Mostly because I know what I'm willing and not willing to give you. I know that if you ever cared about me, you'd be in a risky place, but I own it."

I stare at him, hating how fragile I feel right now. I don't even know what to say.

"But even knowing that I'm better to you than that asshole. I don't expect you shoving your tongue down my throat. I don't expect you to leave work for me. I don't have *any* expectations and that's more than he can say as your fucking ex."

"You curse a lot," I murmur.

"You, you're something else, you know? The most adorable, quirky girl I've ever crossed paths with. And it suits you," he says with a grin, his charming bad-boy vibes adding an enticing edge to his words. "It's a nice break from bloodshed."

I bite my lip as he goes back to cooking. I have no idea what he's making, but I don't care. He eats my cupcakes, so this is nothing.

"How old were you the first time you saw death?"

"Hmm ... I was twelve," he answers, unbothered. "I didn't kill anyone until I was seventeen. It was necessary. I thought I'd hesitate, but I guess I felt like I had to step into the huge shoes my father and older brother left for me. Edmon's first kill was after mine."

"Oh?" I ask, not sure if I should go down this rabbit hole with him.

"Yeah. I've known how to use guns since I was a kid. Knives came later. I prefer guns. I feel better with some distance, I guess. If you ever see me shirtless, you'll see what I mean."

"And ... um ..." I clear my throat, trying to shake the image of him shirtless from my head. "I forgot what I was going to stay."

"Get distracted by something?"

"Maybe," I grumble.

"New rule. If your mind is in the gutter, you share."

"Heck, no!" I argue back. "Absolutely not. That's just a gateway to.."

He turns around and rests his hands on either side of my thighs. I push them together, trying to make my legs smaller. I don't want him to see how thick my thighs are. I don't want him to realize why people don't believe we're together.

"To what?"

I take an unsteady breath. "You're really close."

"What does that do to your mind, huh? Thinking of more than me shirtless?" he asks.

I push against his chest, but all I feel is hard muscle. I suck in another breath and look up at him. He runs his fingers over the outside of my thigh. "No, you're not turned on. You're anxious. Stop being self-conscious around me."

"Because it's fake," I say. "Right?"

"Because you're gorgeous and trust me, my mind is in the gutter at least double the time yours is in there," he says.

I argue, but he grabs my legs and jerks me closer, wrapping my legs around him. Our faces are too close. He's so warm, he's so attractive, so intense and he's right here, looking at me in a way that Aaron never did. Aaron would just hit on me, or say he wanted sex, but Danya, he's staring at me like he can't imagine anything better than having me right here against him.

"Don't tease me or lie to me. We're alone, you don't have to touch me if you don't-"

"I *want* to touch you. I *want* to kiss you. I rarely do things I don't want to do, Abigail. And you ... I want you every damn day."

I study his face, searching for any sign of dishonesty. There's none.

"That's not fake," I say.

"No, it's not. But you want fake. You want simple, and that's what I can give you," Danya says, even though his nose brushes mine and I can feel his breath on my lips. "You want this to be fake so we can walk away and I understand that."

I want that. I should think of the future, I usually do. I always make sure I'm safe and set. I want to make sure that no matter what, I can stay independent and avoid being hurt.

Still, tasting him sounds so much better than being smart right now. Danya's fingers continue up my thigh as his other hand strokes the back of my neck until I shiver. My eyes almost close. "That feels good."

"How good, Cupcake?"

"Good enough that I want to be stupid."

"Is it stupid if it's what you want?" he asks.

My lips brush his. "It's just ... just a few weeks."

"That's all," Danya agrees. "Totally fake other than kisses."

"And just kisses. That's all," I insist.

"Sure, sure. Rules later," he agrees.

We kiss, slowly. I suck his bottom lip, then open for more. I like kissing Danya. The way our tongues move, the way he sucks my tongue, nibbles my bottom lip, and we just keep drawing it out. Danya's fingers slide up into my hair and tighten, jerking my hair back. The little bit of pain makes his soft, warm, eager kisses better.

"Remember that frosting comment I made?" he asks against my lips.

"Yes," I sigh.

"It was definitely about putting frosting on you and licking it off," he growls, before biting my bottom lip. He draws back, taking my lip with him until my lip slips free. I shudder and lean forward for another kiss, just as whatever's on the stove pops angrily.

He pecks my lips and pulls away. "I better cook. I have to impress you with more than my kissing skills."

I don't bother to tell him he's impressed me plenty. He has. The way he stayed cool under literal gunfire, how easily he spoke to me and kept me calm during that whole thing, how he took care of me right after even though were strangers, how immediately and unflinchingly he agreed to be my fake-boyfriend. All of it has impressed me.

As far as boyfriend material, Danya's the total package. He's caring, protecting, and willing to do plenty with me. I shudder and kick my feet until Danya finishes cooking.

We eat together and when the silence has gone on for too long, Danya picks me up and puts me on his lap. I push against him. "Danya!"

"I want you here. Eat," he orders, before holding a fork for me.

I narrow my eyes at him. Why is he encouraging me to eat? Aren't guys supposed to tell me not to? Danya arches an eyebrow. "Are you saying you don't like my food?"

"It's good," I argue.

"That's right, so eat."

I laugh and eat, obeying him. He grins and feeds us both, then puts on a movie. He checks his watch for a second and I glance over at him. "Do you need to go?"

"Nope, making sure that it's not eight," he answers.

Yup, boyfriend material and a tremendous step up from my last boyfriend. I bite my lip. It's fake. There's a time limit. That's it. Simple.

Even if a part of me already, after two dates and less than a week, wants to keep this confusing mess of a man.

NINE

Danya
————

WEDNESDAY, I HEAD BACK TO THE BAKERY. IT'S ON THE WAY to Lev's after bugging Misha's house and car. When I get there, Aaron's nowhere to be seen, but that doesn't mean I can skip out on fake-boyfriend duties. I'd love to get more kisses or spend some time with Abby. It'll just sell the relationship better when Aaron pokes his nose back in Abby's business. If I enjoy it, so be it.

Even though I shouldn't want that, I do. It's stupid. I feel like an idiot for wanting more time with her. After all, it's fake and I'm not looking for love or a relationship or anything like that. I don't want to want to be around her.

When I get to the bakery, Mona sees me, lifts the door, and motions to the back. I head to the kitchen and find Abby making frosting and dancing. I watch for a moment, loving how she dances to nothing at all without music. When she spins, I pick up the dance, continuing to twirl her, then pull her against me.

She giggles. "What are you doing here?"

"Visiting my fake girlfriend, so I get to learn the secrets of her frosting making," I tease.

She blushes. "We are *not* doing the frosting thing you mentioned."

"Of course not, Mona can walk in and that would break a rule," I tease, kissing her nose before I can stop myself. "Nice to know you're not as innocent as you look."

"I told you I'm not a virgin. I'm not some innocent little girl like everyone thinks. I'm powerful," Abby says while flexing her arms.

I laugh, unable to stop resists. "How dare you tempt me."

She giggles and turns around, swiping some of the frosting on her finger. She offers it to me. "I'm worried these strawberries are a little too ripe. You don't like sweet, so you'll tell me."

I lick her finger, then suck it, watching her lips part. The frosting is perfect, as I expected, but I hesitate. "I'm not sure. Let me try it again."

"What? But-"

I dip her thumb into the frosting, then–still holding her wrist–make her put it against her lips. "Suck it off."

She blushes this time, two shades of pink deeper than the color of the frosting. She sucks her thumb, her eyes on me until I feel my cock stir. Her cheeks hollow. Those gorgeous brown eyes stay on me as she pops off her own thumb. Before she can lick her lips, I steal a kiss.

Frosting tastes better on her. She gasps, but grabs my hips, not just my shirt this time. I press her back against the counter and kiss her deeper, my tongue sliding along hers as she moans and kisses me back.

Every flick of her tongue, the way she changes the angle to get the most of each touch and every renewed kiss, drives me crazy. This is the first girl to ever know who I am and what I'm capable of and still kiss me like I'm not some scary monster.

Groaning, I let my hand slide down to her ass and grip

one cheek hard, despite her jeans. She jumps a little, but ends up rubbing herself against me. I nip her tongue. Then she sucks mine. I'm hard, my cock rubbing against her belly until she draws back and looks down. I grip her hair, making her stare at me.

"Is that your gun?" she asks.

I grin. "I think you know the answer to that, don't you, Cupcake?"

"It's ... bigger than I ..." her eyes widen and she swats my chest. "Daniel! This is my kitchen, not some kind of ...."

"You're so damn cute. Feed me more kisses and you'll feel it get harder," I promise.

She turns around, but her ass rubs my cock and I grip her sides. "You're testing my restraint."

"No sex," she reminds me in a breathy voice.

"That doesn't sound like a firm rule," I murmur before kissing the back of her neck. "Lucky for you, I want you to beg for that. I won't give you my cock otherwise."

"Pull it out and I'll cover it in frosting. That's all you get," she grumbles.

I chuckle and kiss her neck again. Something clatters to the table and then her hand is on my hip. "You ..." I keep kissing, noticing the goosebumps on her neck. She tries again. "Danya, please. I have .... I have to focus. I'm the only baker."

That makes me pause. I draw back and she glances over her shoulder at me. My brow furrows. "You make *everything*? Every day?"

"Yes. I told you I'm a perfectionist. Do you think I'd let anyone else work in my kitchen?"

"I think you should. You deserve a life outside of the bakery. I mean, you should have a real life. You should go see friends, enjoy the beach, make the most of Miami."

"You just want me to have a later bedtime," she argues.

I roll my eyes. "No, you're missing out on life."

"Semantics."

"Bullshit, you mean," I huff.

She points at me. "You are going to make my kitchen dirty."

"Is that a request?"

"Boss, there's some lady here for you. Something about a wedding cake?" Mona says before she sees me. She covers her smirk. "And this doesn't look very fake to me."

"Send her in!" Abby answers in a high-pitched voice.

I swat her ass, and she yips, jumping and turning to hide her ass from me. I narrow my eyes at her. "You owe me a kiss. I didn't tell," I growl. "You weren't supposed to tell anyone we were fake." "If it gets out now, Cupcake, it's all on you."

"Mona is allowed to know! She'd never tell Aaron. Don't you spank me," she orders.

"Why? Because you liked it?" I ask with a grin. "I bet you'd like it even more without all that denim in the way."

"You're a butt head."

"I'll take that as a yes, Cupcake."

"Well, don't you two look cute," Sienna says, looking between us. Lev gives me a look after taking off his sunglasses. Sienna rubs Lev's chest. "Abby, this is my husband to be. I've been gushing about you nonstop since the party and he'd love to do a tasting. We can do the strawberry chocolate, but also the cookies and cream."

"Sure! I have cupcakes available in both and I'm working on another round of the strawberry frosting," she says, ignoring me.

Yup, I don't like that. And I don't like that I want her attention either. I need to back up. I need to back off and get my head on straight. Maybe getting laid will fix it? Maybe getting to take out Misha will calm whatever is currently going crazy in me.

Sienna walks out, but Lev lingers. He looks at me, then

at Abby. I step between them and switch the conversation to Russian. "What?"

"Thought you didn't want to end up like Ed, me, and dad," he answers.

"I'm not. I'm doing Abby a favor thanks to your fiancée," I respond.

"Doesn't seem like there's a threat here. She doesn't even have anyone else working with her," he says.

"You don't know the details. It's not your business."

"You're the brother that keeps pointing out people shouldn't know who or what we are," he argues.

"She was there the night the cartel came in. She dropped a man on her own and attacked me with a frying pan. She put all the pieces together and is happy to pretend it's not real. She's not like ..." I stop myself when I realize how ridiculous I sound.

"Forget it. I'll join you two in a second," I answer.

Lev smirks and switches to English. "No need, little brother. Enjoy your girlfriend."

I flip him off, but see Abby shaking.

I wrap my arms around her and kiss her neck. Her pulse is thundering, and I know she's uncomfortable. I rub her sides. "Take a breath, Abby."

"Another event where .... where things can happen. Things that only belong in nightmares, Daniel," she whispers.

"It won't happen like that again. I promise,"

"You can't promise that. If you could, I wouldn't know you and I'd be fending off my ex all by myself." I notice she hesitates when she says it though. Something tells me that at this point, she might have taken him back. He wouldn't be this determined if she'd kicked him to the curb. I kiss the top of her head. She pushes me away. "Go on. I have to prepare for this."

"Cupcake-"

"I'm serious, Daniel. I don't need your services today," she says, standing her ground.

If she was this fierce with her ex, I'd be impressed, but I don't appreciate it turned on me. Still, I walk out to the front of the shop and continue to the street. Abby's right. We're not in a relationship. I don't know why I keep letting myself forget that when I'm with her. I should have turned around and walked away when I saw Aaron wasn't here. There was no reason for me to go in, no reason for me to tease her in the back, to kiss her, to keep teasing myself with having more than a kiss.

Abby handled one night of my reality and I don't want to end up like my brothers or my father, chained to some-one, willing to put them first when that's not the life. We're mafia first, foremost, and only. They forgot that. I haven't.

Even if Abby could be a hell of an asset. I bet she'd poison someone who threatened those she cared about. She'd beat someone else with a frying pan. She'd tell me how to fix wounds. She could be an asset, but I know that I wouldn't be able to control myself around her and she'd cry anytime someone died.

She's too soft-hearted. She's too sweet.

Which is why I have to let her go. I can't keep holding onto her. I can't let this continue. I'll just wait for her to text me when she needs me.

I glance back into the shop and see her serving my brother and Sienna. Her eyes flick to me, then away as she turns pink. I almost groan. I want to go back in and stake my claim on her, but that's stupid, just like she said when I made her dinner and she kissed me.

Three kisses, six times jerking off to her, and too much time spent on a girl who can't handle my life or better it. Until I find my very own mafia queen, I will not settle down. Abby isn't that person and I will not turn her life upside down to make her that person. It's simple.

That's what I tell myself as I force myself into my car. Even though I want to go in there and find every excuse to touch her, to make her smile, to claim Abby as mine, I won't. I know that's stupid. It's my damn lust talking and nothing else.

My brothers can live their happily ever after and I'll throw myself into the ocean to fight a bull shark to avoid being tempted by Abby again.

Taking on a bull shark will end better than allowing myself to be alone with her again. Sweetness is a weakness that we can't afford. So I'll figure out how to get through the rest of this week with a lot of talk and no action.

When I look down at my hands on the steering wheel, I realize my fingers are crossed.

"Fucking hell," I curse softly.

TEN

Abigail
———————

THE BAKERY IS SLOW FOR THE REST OF THE DAY. I'M NOT sure if it's because Sienna and her husband to be, Lev, are here, or if their scary man outside is driving people away. I offer them multiple different options and glance at Mona more than once, but Mona's focused elsewhere. She licks her lips as she looks at the man standing outside.

"Just go," I encourage her. "Show him your moves."

Mona winks at me. "I guess I'll take my break."

"This one," Lev says, pointing at a cupcake.

Sienna giggles. "I knew it would be your favorite."

They kiss and he rubs up her thigh. She grabs his wrist and shakes her head, despite her bright eyes flicking to me and then back to him. She whispers in his ear and he groans. "Four tiers of the chocolate and strawberry."

"But!" Sienna jumps up and moves around the table even though her fiancé looks like he's about to jump up and pull her down on the table and to enjoy her right here, no matter who sees. She holds a hand out to Lev, like she's fending him off. "But can you also do filling in the cake?"

"More chocolate?" Lev guesses.

"No, something light. Like whipped cream or a mascarpone with strawberries?" Sienna answers while still edging away from her fiancé.

"Whatever you want," he agrees, his voice low and growly.

"It sounds like it's settled. Anything in terms of décor?" I ask.

"We'll send it over," Lev decides, his eyes only on his bride- to- be. "Right now, my fiancée and I have something to take care of."

"Is that so? I was thinking I'd go into greater detail with Abby on a few of the specifics and touch base on-"

In one move, she's over his shoulder. She gasps and waves to me. "I'll send over some inspiration photos I have with specifics!"

"Okay!" I yell, waving as he carries her out of the building. I've never seen a couple more in love or more willing to show it. It's cute, especially considering that Lev's in the mafia. I wouldn't even guess that he was involved in crime just by looking at him with Sienna.

It's like the fact he's in the mafia doesn't matter at all to her. She just *loves* him. As he is. For some reason, knowing that weighs on my mind. Rather than worrying about it, I work on cleaning up the table, making sure to think about what Sienna and Lev will want on their cake. I doubt they'll do the actual little people statues that have fallen out of fashion.

Maybe they'll want flowers. I could imagine some gold leaf on the flowers to add some extra class, maybe some gems to make it sparkle a bit. The idea makes me smile. I sketch a few things, send them over, and Sienna sends me her goals ideas–a look of pearls (white and gold) alongside some fun texturing of the frosting. I put small purple flowers into the mix, cascading and wrapping around the cake.

Grinning, I order what I'll need on top of the usual ingredients for my pastries. I spend the rest of the day baking and prepping for tomorrow, so I can sleep soon. When we close up, I almost expect Danya to be waiting for me outside, but he's not.

I tell myself everything is going to be fine, then nod. I told him I need time, and that's what he's going to give me. Even if I wish he wouldn't. I roll my eyes and get on my vespa. This is the right thing to do. Kissing in private leads to doing a lot more in private. I have to remember the bloodshed, his warning about me being in danger by being with him, and the very real ramifications of being with him. I could die. I'd always be in danger. I doubt I'd ever get to sleep around my bed time. I could die!.

Shaking my head, I throw myself back into work over the next few days. I don't text Danya, I don't ask for him to come around, but I leave a bit earlier to go to a restaurant on the beach, basking in the sea breeze.

Maybe I should get an assistant. I could teach someone in the kitchen, hire them part time just to see how they do and consider hiring them full time or something like that. I smile at the thought as I take a drink from my margarita. I lick the salt from the rim and let my head fall back a bit.

"Well, a woman like you shouldn't be alone," a tan man with dark hair and warm brown eyes says with a grin. "And you shouldn't be limited to one drink."

"Thank you, but I'm enjoying the quiet."

"More than you'd enjoy some time with company?" he asks before purring to me in Spanish.

We talk for a bit and I have another margarita, one that feels a lot stronger than the first. I hesitate as I get halfway through the first sip and my eyes flick to the man. "What did you say your name was? It skipped out of my head."

"Oh, me? I'm no one but a handsome face to keep a ... beautiful woman company. Hermosa princesa," he croons.

"So no names, just sharing a table?" I ask.

He nods.

"Do you mind if I get a picture of the ocean? I want to send it to my friend who's stuck at work, just to make her a little jealous," I say.

He nods. I lift my camera and get half of his face in the photo. I send it to Danya just because I don't like the way this guy talks or how he avoids basic questions. After a few minutes, my phone buzzes.

The man grabs my hand. "Your friend must be very jealous to text back so fast."

"Of course she is. She doesn't get to see the beach very often," I say with a grin before answering my phone.

He's asking for a location. That isn't a good sign. I send the restaurant name and put my phone down. "Don't worry, I told her I'm with good company and don't want to be disturbed."

For some reason, knowing that a murderous man is on his way to save me has me grinning instead of panicking. I keep the conversation going and when the man says we should get some food to enjoy while drinking, I agree. I order the tempura shrimp with the sweet chili sauce and he stares at me.

"A woman who can handle her heat?" he asks.

"Oh, of course. I'm very familiar with hot ... things," I say, trying to steer my mind away from Danya, eating with him, kissing him, feeling him against me. "Plus, with this amazing margarita, beautiful view, and good company, I think we can handle a little heat."

"I like the way you think," he says with a wolfish smile. "It might be even more fun to get out of here."

I twirl my hair, smile, then take another drink of the margarita. "That's tempting."

"Is it?"

"There's just this thing ..." I trace the rim of my glass and suck the salt from my finger. My phone buzzes in my purse, but I ignore it to meet the man's eyes. There's something dark in his gaze. I know it after my time with my ex. I know it after seeing the eyes of some men my father represents.

"Oh? What thing is that? Don't tell me you have an overprotective, untrusting boyfriend who wouldn't allow you to go to the beach or to a club with a new friend," he says, leaning his head to the side and pursing his lips.

It's a challenge. If I say yes, I'm being trained or manipulated. If I say no, then I don't have a boyfriend who will come to protect me. Either way, he gets an answer on if I'm willing to proceed, if I'm single, if he can whisk me away. If he wasn't glancing around every five seconds like someone's going to show up and drive him away, if he hadn't just sat down without a name, with no information about himself, I might believe he's a good man.

But that glint in his eyes, the way he's so nervous about my phone, the line of questions ...

"So?"

"I have a thing about secondary locations," I laugh as I say it, as if I find it silly myself. "I guess it's all the true crime my friend watches. I never want to go somewhere after being one place. It just doesn't seem... safe or wise, you know?"

"Really? Then how do you ever date?"

"I go one place–driving myself there to the place we agree on–and meet with the person. We say good bye at that place and I go home alone. After a few dates, I'll let them come over," I answer with a shrug. "It's okay, it's a girl thing to worry about secondary locations and being alone with a stranger, no matter how handsome, charming, or funny they are."

"So you think I'm handsome, charming, and funny?" he asks, leaning forward.

I wink at him. I know how to make a man feel like he's in charge. It's how I survived a year with Aaron without having to replace entire walls, just little fist- sized holes. That's why I'm not questioning my gut, that's why I sucked up my pride and every rational thought that's trying to tell me to walk away from Danya and texted him, just to make sure someone is here to keep me safe.

Just as my next margarita arrives–without me asking for it–and the food is put down, a few fingers stroke over my shoulder, delicate. His palm grazes my neck as the man in front of me loses every trace of kindness that was in his expression, glowers at me.

"Oh, Cupcake, are you drunk already?" Danya croons.

I look up at him and smile. I'm tipsy because his hand on the back of my neck, rubbing and teasing my skin feels so good, so perfect, that I think I'm wet from that touch alone, from the sharpness in his glacial eyes. His jaw tightens as he looks at the man I'm sitting with.

"Thank you for keeping my girlfriend safe. She can be a little wild when she drinks," Danya says, his thumb and fingers digging into the back of my neck. "I'd be happy to pay for everything, your tab as well."

"I didn't realize she had a boyfriend, considering she's here alone," the man says in a low, threatening voice.

"How could you have known?"

"How could you cross the line?. I know you killed my-"

Danya speaks Spanish, sharp, decisive, unforgiving, but he puts his free hand on the table, moving the knife off it. I bend down, pick up the knife and the fork that's down there, but keep the knife in my lap.

The man stands up and lifts his shirt, flashing a gun. His eyes flick to me as I make myself sit there. I won't shake. I won't be afraid. I won't move or run or anything else. I'm planted in this seat. I reach forward and take one shrimp, popping it into my mouth as I hold the tail. I watch the stranger as I bite down, set the tail down, chew, and swallow.

I take a slow drink of my margarita and smile. "Secondary locations are a no, Cielo."

His lip curls and he walks away. Danya's hand slides along my jaw and he lifts my chin. "How much of that did you understand?"

"None. I only know the basics and some pet names in Spanish," I answer.

"Good. You should learn some Russian too," he mumbles.

"Why would I do that?" I ask.

"I have my reasons," he answers. He leans down. "This one is a necessity, Abby."

He kisses me, drawing it out, but denying me plenty. His tongue only teases mine, doesn't go any deeper. After that, he takes the other guy's seat. "What are we having while you get trashed?"

ELEVEN

Danya

ABBY FINISHES HER THIRD MARGARITA, NOT HOLDING BACK AT all. She sets the knife back on the table and takes a few quick breaths. "I don't want the shrimp."

"You're eating or you're not driving," I say.

She texted me because she knew, she knew something was wrong with the guy. I don't want her to only reach out when she's convinced that she needs me. Even if that's what's necessary for us to both live functioning lives. The days without her have been driving me crazy. I want her to want me the same way I want her, in every possible way and in every possible position.

"You caught on to that trick with the knife," I note.

"It was obvious," she answers before circling the top of her glass and sucking the salt off her drink. "I've started coming here this week instead of going right home. I think I've been to half the restaurants up and down the coast."

"You have?"

"Mmhmm. And I've considered hiring someone to bake on a trial, part-time basis. If they follow the recipes, if they do well and don't try changing things, then I might just make it a full-time thing ... maybe," she continues. "What have you been up to?"

"Working out, doing things you wouldn't want to hear about." It's easy to dismiss. I have a few pieces of shrimp just to do something and Abby eats as well. I exhale a breath I didn't realize I was holding. "I'm glad you're spending more time out of the bakery."

"I love the bakery, you know? Sometimes I wonder if cooking would calm me as much, but I don't think it would. They say cooking is all about doing things with your heart, about seasoning to taste, about enjoying the moment and making what you want, but baking has rules. I think I like rules."

I smile. "Is that why you sent me away?"

She pauses, reaches for her margarita, and pulls out the lemon. She plays with it for a second, then sucks it, not even making a face despite how sour it is. She sighs. "I sent you away because there are times where you scare me."

"Do I?"

"Knowing what you do for a living, hearing how you talk to your brother, thinking of being put back in a position with violence. A bloody, violent situation, it kind of popped the very attractive, very hot bubble I find myself in whenever you're around."

"Oh, I put you in a bubble?" I can't help the smirk that turns up my lips.

She considers that and leans back in her chair. She fans herself. "I'm hot. That's the trouble with Florida. There's no getting used to or escaping the heat. Lived here my whole life and right now, I wish I was in a bikini and nothing else."

God, even drunk, the woman knows how to distract the hell out of me. I can picture her in a string bikini, her tits falling out. Not just a bikini, one of those sexy thong bikinis, so next to all of her is on display. Those big brown eyes on me, leaning closer and closer until her plush lips are on mine and ...

"Ugh. I don't want another one. Can I have some water?" she asks the waiter.

He clears his throat. "I was told to keep the margaritas coming."

I expect Abby to just let it go, like she does with so much, but she doesn't. She grabs his wrist and makes him look at her. "I'm the one drinking. I never asked for more than one. I want water. Just water. No ice. No lemon. Water."

When he doesn't answer, but tries to leave, she holds him in place, refusing to look away. "Repeat what I just said, so I know that's what I'm getting."

"Just water. No ice. No lemon. Water," he answers, his voice shaking.

"I have special nail polish on, too. Why do you think I didn't finish the second margarita? I dumped half of it out," she says without a trace of the sweetness I've heard from her. She smiles. "Trust me when I tell you, I won't be the one to hurt you if I act strange. And the man that left me here without a name, with nothing but a few fake smiles, he's nothing compared to the connections I have."

She let him go with a smile so sweet that I can't believe the tone she just used. "So, just one water and the check."

He hurries away and I arch an eyebrow. She rolls out her neck. "Alcohol is liquid courage, isn't it?"

"Where did you just pull that from?" I ask.

"I've learned plenty, but I'd rather be sweet. Once a girl is mean or rude, that's all she is in someone's eyes. She's manipulative, too smart, too outspoken. It's easier to be smaller, sweeter, gentler. It's easier to be the person I want to be and try to see the world as a good place instead of admitting its terrible. It's easier to ... get through bad times with some cupcakes and move forward."

Who the hell is Abby? She's so much more than some baker who doesn't know herself. That's fucking obvious right now. So is the intense attraction sizzling across my skin. I couldn't bring some innocent, too sweet woman into my hell, but this side of her, who uses her sweetness as a fucking weapon, she can handle it.

"You're going to finish your water, I'm going to pay the check, and we're leaving," I decide.

Her eyes widen and she sucks her bottom lip. "Why?"

"Because it's my job to get you home safe, Cupcake."

"But you ...."

"Do you want more time? Do you want me to leave?"

She watches me, looks to the right, her cheeks flair pink, but she clears her throat. "I got more instructions for the cake. I'm working on a mascarpone now. I've never made one before."

"Abby," I say. "Do you want me to leave?"

"I didn't say that," she insists. "I didn't say that I want you to leave."

"Then what do you want, Cupcake?. You're in control here, even if you're wasted," I say with a smirk.

She giggles. "I don't know. Honestly, I kind of missed you, even if you can be annoying and intense and far too sexual."

"Annoying and intense are fair, but I think I'm just a little too repressed," I tease, reaching my foot out under the table until it touches hers. "And I think you feel it, too."

"You're terrible. Taking advantage of drunk women like this," she teases while looking up at me through her dark lashes. "You should behave."

"Oh Cupcake," I groan. "I can never behave around you."

The man brings her water. I pay the bill, and she downs it. She lets me take her home. At her door, I hesitate. The reason I agreed to walk away, beyond her saying that's what she wanted, was because she's distracting me from my job–my life having feelings is a weakness. It is. I know that, but didn't she just prove she's a lot more than she seems?

Plus, she's going to the wedding. There's no way she'll just send the cake and not go. Which means she's wrapped up in our life until then. Is there any real point in resisting Abby?

"That kiss earlier was the first fake one you've given me, isn't it?" She asks while playing with her keys.

"Yes," I answer.

"I didn't like it. Tasted a lot like restraint."

"That's all it was," I agree.

"Then I demand a do over." I think she actually stomps her foot as she says it.

I chuckle, wrap my arm around her waist, and jerk her towards me. She giggles and strokes my face. "I kind of like your scruff."

"You do?" I arch an eyebrow. "Where else do you want to feel my scruff or my lips?"

She nibbles her lip, then grabs my shirt in both fists. "Are you going to kiss me, or do I have to kiss you?"

I lean down to follow through, my nose brushing hers, but my phone rings. I close my eyes a second, debating if I can put it off, but Lev doesn't call for something that can wait and since it's his ring tone, I have little choice..

"Please, don't move," I beg.

She pouts at me as I take the call. I switch to Russian to avoid killing the mood. "What is it?"

"Kill him. Kill him now. I have four more names. All gone. Tonight," Lev blurts. "One of Misha's lackies made a move on Lilah today."

"He didn't expect Ed?"

"Stephanie and Lilah are very effective when it comes to taking a man out. He's already sitting in booking. I have texted addresses to you. Move immediately," Lev demands.

I hang up and kiss the top of Abby's head. "Do me a favor and I promise to give you whatever you want."

"What is it? I don't sign unless I know the fine print," she whispers.

"Stay inside. Do not leave. Do not text me. And if someone knocks-"

"I have a bat I can use on someone," she says. "And the frying pan. I have a big cast iron skillet too. Maybe I could-"

I hold her face between my hands and kiss her. "You're going to get me killed by turning me on like this. Hide. Call the police, and if they get in, make them regret it."

"And I get whatever I want?"

"Within reason. I have limits," I say before swatting her ass. "Inside, now."

"Okay. Be safe. I can't do needles, remember?"

With that, she goes inside and I don't know if it's my cock hardening or my heart racing that has me more distracted. I'm not sure I'm going to be able to clear my head, but once I get to the first address, all distractions are gone.

If I fail, my brothers are in danger, innocent people are in danger, and Abby, a somewhat-innocent, semi-sweet Abby, will be in danger. Considering the asshole who cornered her at the restaurant, she's already in danger, which means that low-ranking cartel man who showed up and sat with her drinking. He is on the hit list too.

The first two men are easy enough to take out. I stage one scene. Don't bother to stage the other since I know I'm not leaving any evidence behind. Then I get to Misha's place and see Ed with a bruise on his face and blood splattered on his shoulder.

"You're getting a little sloppy, brother," I tease him.

He shoves me. "Want to scare him out back so I get the kill?"

"Whatever makes this fastest," I say.

"Alright, head in, I'll cover the back and-"

Bullets come flying out of the front windows and I shove him down, taking one to the forearm. I hiss between my teeth and glower at him. Ed shoves me. "What, I can't take my own bullets?"

"Lilah's been through enough," I groan. "That's a fucking rude hello."

"Make them pay for it?" Ed asks.

"Like we said, let's make it fast."

Ed nods and we go to my trunk. He pulls out some tech we shouldn't have. With one move, we can see every living human in the house all lit up in red. I grin at my twin and he grins right back.

"Think we'll be done before dinner?"

"Who knows, rabbits run. We will finish before dawn," I grumble.

We load up, happy we're in a neighborhood where those uninvolved get out of the way but don't bother with police, then get to work. Shooting fish in a barrel is only slightly harder than shooting cowards camping in a foreclosed home.

TWELVE

Abigail

I WATCH T.V. WITH MY BAT CLOSE AND MY LARGEST CAST iron skillet in my lap. At least twice I realize I should call the police, or that I should turn Danya in., but considering the kind of people that he and his family handle, it seems better to let them do what has to be done, even if Danya's working is outside the law.

Not rational thinking, I admit that. My dad wouldn't call it close to plausible deniability and my mother would be horrified. Their sweet daughter all wrapped up in business she shouldn't know about, let alone be a part of.

It should bother me that a man I like, a man I was begging to steal a kiss from less than three hours ago, just went to kill someone, or multiple someones, but he was honest about it. He's never hidden his giant red flags.

After a bit, I get through a shower, keeping my weapons close, then change for bed, pulling on a giant t-shirt that slides down my shoulder and some comfortable cotton shorts that are too short for my ass not to hang out.

An alarm on my phone goes off and I stare at it. "Huh. Two weeks is up, Danya. No more pretend boyfriend duties."

Does that mean he won't come back? No, he didn't set an alarm telling him when to be done with me. He's not that anal. He already said he didn't like rules. But still. I play with my fingers.

Two hard thuds echo through my door and I grab my skillet, leaving my bat behind the couch. As I stand against the door, I remember when I was little and my dad told me that we were going to play a game, a game that meant I couldn't be seen in windows and had to sneak around the house like a spy.

Later, Mom said it was because he lost a big case and he didn't want the press to see me. Something about the way she said it, slurring her words thanks to alcohol, made me question it then, but now I wonder if Dad was hiding me from someone worse. Was I always going to end up either with or running from someone like Danya or running from them?

"Open. The. Door.," Danya's voice orders.

I open it and he falls to the floor. He groans. There's blood on him–guess it's good he wore black–he's in pain. His twin stands at the door. "Did my job, brother. Now I have my own woman to see to."

"Yeah, yeah."

"Oh, nice to meet you again-kinda. I'm Edmon," the twin says, smiling, and reaching forward to shake my hand. "Your cupcakes are amazing."

"Mine," Danya says, swatting at his twin's hand. "This is *my* woman. Go to yours."

"Touchy-touchy. Knew it wasn't fake. Worst lie I've ever heard," Edmon says before walking out and shutting the door, hitting Danya's foot on the way out.

I try to pick Danya up and he helps me, wrapping an arm around my shoulder as I get him to his feet. "Have you thought about what you want?"

"You don't get to ask that in your shape. We're starting

with a shower. Yes, you're going to use soap," I decide, turning the water on. I test it twice as Danya takes his shirt off.

Seeing him shirtless, *finally*, is ruined considering he's got a huge bruise coming in on his side and he's pink with blood. Danya steps closer. "Want to watch me undo my pants, too?"

"*Can* you undo your pants yourself?" I breathe. "I don't know how injured you are."

He sits down on the toilet and takes off his shoes. He reaches for them, winces, and moves his shoes to the side. I take care of his socks and realize I'm on my knees in front of him. God, it would be so easy to take this in a different, not appropriate direction.

Danya grins at me as I undo his belt. "You're blushing. I think your mind's right back in the gutter, Cupcake."

"Shush, you're hurt," I grumble.

"Later, Abby," he croons, reaching down and cupping my chin. He strokes over my bottom lip with his thumb. "I promise, this won't be your only memory of me shirtless."

"Yup, because you're getting in the shower. I think you can leave your boxers on," I mumble, standing up. I take his hands and pull him up with me.

He arches his eyebrow. "You sound very sure my ass isn't injured."

My mouth opens and closes. Danya holds my shoulder in one hand, then the back of my head in the other. "Strip me, Abby."

"But ... you're injured."

"You want me to use the soap? You're either going to be extra sweet and whisper 'please' against my lips, or you're going to strip me," he growls.

My stomach does flips. I stroke down his sides and drag his boxers down, making myself watch his face and *only* his face even as my breathing hitches and I'm afraid I'm going to moan or whimper.

Danya grins and takes a step forward. "Now the 'please'."

"But you said ..." I take an uneven breath. There's no point in arguing with him. "Please get in the shower?"

His lips brush mine, then he bites my bottom lip and pulls me against him. A low growl leaves his throat as he kisses me with an insatiable hunger, his tongue entwined with mine, while his fingers weave through my hair. Every scalding kiss and possessive touch makes me forget everything but *us*.

Danya pushes me back against a wall and his kisses become desperate, his hands exploring the contours of my body. He tugs at my shirt, revealing the warmth of my skin. I gasp and pull away. I push against his hand. "No, I'm ..."

"Gorgeous, mine, wonderful," he growls against my lips. He continues in Russian, gripping the back of my neck as our tongues tangle and brush. Danya grips my hip, jerking me against him. "Mine."

"But ..." I draw back to free my mouth, even though kissing him seems so much better. "Shower. Blood. Too much blood!"

"Sorry." he steps back and shakes his head. "Shower."

"Yeah," I whisper.

He gets in the shower and I almost peek. I'm close to pulling the curtain to the side just to check him out when I hear him slip. I gasp and jerk the curtain off the wall, nearly taking myself out.

Danya is unbothered. The water around his feet is red, but I don't look. He's right here, naked, muscle on muscle. His impressive cock is thick, long, and curving slightly toward me like it wants to be down my throat.

"Couldn't stop yourself?" he asks.

"Danya, you're ..." I can't drag my eyes away from his

body, and most notably, his cock. Oh, my mouth is watering and I'm so wet, I'm sure he's going to know.

"This is a side effect of being around you, let alone kissing you, cupcake. Didn't trust me to wash myself?"

"I ... you slipped!" I say, my voice all kinds of high and ridiculous. "I heard you slip."

"I can handle gunfire, plenty of violence, you think I'm going to let a tub-"

He slips and somehow lands on top of me. I have his chest, now clean of blood, right in front of me. Danya pants. "You did this."

"Yeah. I know what I want," I decide.

He touches my face. "It better involve nothing but your bed."

I kiss him hard, wrapping one arm around him to keep him close he groans and I feel his cock between my thighs. My eyes roll back and I try to pull him closer. The hot water is nothing compared to Danya. I moan and keep slipping when I try to wrap my legs around him.

He chuckles and draws back. "Cupcake, you and I need to get out of this tub."

"It's not big enough," I agree.

It takes some work, but Danya gets out, then pulls me up. I notice the bullet wound on his arm and my eyes narrow. "Who shot you!"

"I killed them."

"Good, because those sons of biscuits would have gotten a wasabi and jalapeno cupcake shoved right into their eyes and down their throat," I growl.

Danya jerks me out of the tub and picks me up. I squeal and try to force him to put me down, but instead, he drops me onto my bed. "You're so damn sexy."

"But you ... you ..." I can't get the words out.

"Oh, I'm going to show you plenty, but I cut you off earlier, didn't I?" He asks, his accent a lot stronger than it was earlier. He strokes up my thighs, grabs my shorts and jerks them down. "What is it you wanted?"

"This," I answer.

"You don't get away with a one word answer," he growls lifting my foot and kissing my instep. "I want details. Let's see if you can match my fantasies."

"I want you to kiss every inch of me and ... and," I can hardly get the words out. With Danya's eyes on me, focused on my face with that knowing, wicked smile on his face spreading on his lip, how am I supposed to focus on speaking?

"And?"

"I'll tell you when you get through with part one," I moan.

He groans and pushes my leg to the side, gripping my shirt. I hold it in place too. He tugs, but I shake my head. Danya sighs. "You're making me self-conscious. I'm here, naked on top of you and you won't take off your shirt?"

"I'm ..."

"If you say anything but "mouthwatering", "gorgeous", or possibly "better with frosting", I'm going to be insulted, Abby," he growls, leaning down to kiss me. "You're the sexiest woman in the fucking world."

My cheeks heat as he continues kissing down my neck. "Either let me take this shirt off, or I'm going to tear it off you."

"Danya," I sigh.

"Because I'm not going to fuck you in it. That's morning sex," he says, nibbling my throat. "It's not first time sex."

"You're ... sentimental."

"I'm greedy, Abigail, there's a big difference. Want me to prove it?" he asks, jerking my shirt down to kiss my collarbone.

"As long as you don't stop," I moan. "Don't stop, Danya."

He slowly pulls my shirt up, shifting on me so he kisses up my thigh, over my hip, along my belly, his mouth following every inch of skin revealed as he drags my shirt up. Then he has it over my head.

Danya groans as he cups my breasts, pushing them together, squeezing them. "Fucking flawless."

I moan and pull him down to kiss me as he continues playing with my breasts and teasing me with every touch. He pinches my nipple, making my back arch, then takes the other nipple in his mouth, sucking and flicking his tongue over the hard peak.

"Danya!"

"Just the start, Cupcake," he promises me.

His mouth continues down my body and he spreads my legs wide. I whimper as I feel his breath on my pussy. "I'll have to kiss the rest of you later. I'm very distracted right now."

"Yes," I agree softly.

"Good girl," he answers before licking over my slit. "Delicious and all mine."

I nod, but he doesn't need an answer. He grips my thighs tight and buries his face between them. I moan as his tongue flicks over my clit. I fist the sheet, grab his hair, roll my body against him to have more of his tongue, his lips, everything.

Danya sucks and rolls his tongue over my clit, then adjusts to work his fingers inside me at the same time. The rules were stupid, so stupid. He was right. It's that simple. My eyes roll back as my back arches. His name leaves my lips like a prayer as Danya proves he's good at everything. Killing, flirting, kissing, and so very good with his tongue.

Why would I ever want to let a man like this go?

THIRTEEN

Danya

——————

ABBY TIGHTENS HER LEGS AROUND MY HEAD AS HER HAND curls in my hair, sparking pain and making me groan against her soaked pussy. I lick from her entrance to her clit over and over, softening my tongue each time to make sure she keeps trembling for me.

"Danya. Oh ... Danya," she chants. "No one's ever.."

"If you say no one has ever eaten you out," I warn, grabbing her thighs and prying them off my ears.

She bites her bottom lip as her cheeks go from pink to burning red. "I haven't let anyone else."

"Abby," I groan, feasting on her all over again.

She's so damn sweet and receptive. I love how she arches for my tongue, grips my hair with both hands, pulling me tigter against her delicious pussy. I'd be happy to devour her every single day, eating her out until she's so oversensitive that she's trembling and already on the edge before I can fuck her.

Then again, I also like the idea of starting every day by tasting her pussy, then her moans and finally her fuckin' cupcakes. Abby lifts her hips off the bed to grind against my tongue until she comes apart again.

"Danya, please!" She lets out a soft sob and then hums when I just kiss her clit.

I let her drop down to the bed and push her legs apart further, kissing along her inner thighs, licking across her skin, and nibbling the inside of her knee. "I hope you enjoy being eaten out. I'm not planning to restrain myself again."

"Again?" she asks.

I chuckle and flip her over, biting her ass until she moans and rocks back against me as I palm each butt cheek. I lick and kiss up her spine, then nibble the nape of her neck as I rub my cock against her ass.

"I've wanted to devour you anytime we've been in a kitchen together. I also considered it on that first date. Those table cloths were so long and that dress ... I knew I could push it up to your thighs, spread your legs and make you come right there," I purr in her ear.

"Oh," she whines. "You're kinky."

"You don't know the half of it, Cupcake. I'm being gentle right now. I'll be nice and vanilla right now, but next time ... next time we're going to explore your kinks," I say before nipping her neck.

Abby rolls under me, then wraps her arms around my neck, pulling me down to kiss her. She sucks my lip, licks deeper into my mouth, then reaches between us and strokes my cock. I can feel where she's trying to get me, but I like her words so much more. I *need* to hear how much she wants me.

I fell first. I can admit that to myself, so I need to know that we're on the same page. That she wants me for more reasons than my blatant sex appeal and the fact that she's riding an adrenaline high.

"We got through part one, Abby. What's part two?" I ask before sucking her earlobe.

I continue kissing along her neck as I pull her thigh around my hip. I bite the top of her breast when she doesn't answer, then choke her with one hand as she whimpers and moans for me. Abby gasps and she lifts her chin.

Rubbing my thumb down the front of her neck, I hold her gaze. "Tell me what part two is."

She strokes my cock again, her fingers circling the sensitive head before she rubs her pussy against me. "You know what part two is?"

"Nope. I don't," I tease. "I want to hear you say it."

"I ..." she looks away, but I turn her back to meet my eyes.

"It's just us. I won't let anyone else know what a dirty mind you have," I promise, kissing the corner of her lips. "Tell me, Cupcake."

"I want to taste you too, but ... but I want you inside me more," she whispers. "So I'd like to have sex with you and then have you finish in my mouth."

Fitting my mouth to hers, I kiss her, then deeper as she moans against me. My hand strokes down her throat and I squeeze her breast in my hand. Abby guides me where she needs me, and I thrust deep inside her.

Her back arches against me and her lips part. "Oh!"

Fuck, she's tight, really tight, soaking wet, and so fucking warm. I groan and draw back. She turns her head away, hiding it in her pillow as I draw back and slam into her again, watching her tits bounce, her thighs shake. Having her naked, moaning under me, panting and whimpering as she tries to pull me closer. It's everything I've wanted and more. I can taste her on my tongue even as I set a pace that keeps her moaning, like she can't string two thoughts together while I'm inside her.

"You're better than I dreamed, Abby," I growl against her skin before sucking her nipple between my lips. I suck and lick as she lifts herself off the bed to make the most of me.

Abby meets every thrust, tangles her fingers in my hair

as her other hand strokes down my back to brush me. I chuckle and lick between her breasts and along her neck until she trembles for me.

"Use your words. I'll give you everything you want, everything you need," I pant.

Abby meets my eyes as I slide my hand around the back of her neck, massaging the spot as I slow my pace. I roll my hips and see her eyes dip to my body.

She strokes over my chest and abs, gripping my hips. "You feel good, Danya. Really good," she breathes, a satisfied sound escaping her lips.

A pleased sound leaves my throat.

"So, so good," she continues, her head falling back. "But ..."

"But?" I come to a dead stop and narrow my eyes.

"You're holding back. Stop it. No restraint," she orders.

I chuckle. "I might break you if you do that."

She wiggles against me. "You promised not to stop! You promised to give me what I want. Do it."

With that, I flip her over, jerk her hips back and slam into her. Abby releases a feral moan that has my cock twitching inside her. I swat her ass hard. "You better stay loud for me until my hand is around your throat."

"Yes!" she yells.

Wrapping my hand in her hair, I jerk her back. I want to hear everything. She doesn't get to hide a single moan. I swat her ass again. "That's right. Be loud. Make your fucking neighbors jealous of your pussy."

She moans and pants for me, whimpering when I swat her ass, but never asking me to stop. I love watching her ass jiggle, love watching her skin bloom pink under my hand as she whimpers, moans, yells my name until she falls hoarse.

Abby comes for me again, her pussy trying to suck my cock deeper, so I give it to her, slamming into her until I have nothing more to give, grinding deep inside her as her wetness slicks her thighs and my cock.

I'm still not close. I'm too focused on her, on what she needs to come, again and again and again. I climb half on top of her and push her down against the bed, so I'm between her legs as I hold her down. I grip her breast, kissing the nape of her neck, her jaw, anywhere I can reach as I continue fucking her.

"Danya!" she howls. "Fuck, I can't ... I can't!"

"One more," I growl, feeling my own toes starting to curl and a demanding heat filling my lower belly.

She wraps her arm around my head as her lips part and her eyes roll back. She comes again, gushing for me as her entire body shakes. When she finishes, I jerk out of her as quickly as I can. I don't want to finish inside her and I promised to finish in her mouth. I keep my fucking word.

Abby keeps shaking as I roll her onto her side and offer her my cock, shining with her juices. She opens her eyes as I tap the tip of my dick against her lips. "You want to finish me, Cupcake?"

"Yes," she sighs.

Abby parts her lips and takes my cock. I expect her to stop, to draw back, to have to take her time, but she takes more than half my cock in one go. I groan and tangle my fingers in her hair. Her eyes, all hazy and dilated, flick up to mine as she draws back and teases the head of my cock with her tongue.

"Fuck," I hiss.

She adjusts, grips my ass, then takes me deeper. Her throat tightens around me as she tries to take every thick inch, and she gags. She draws back and does it again, changing the angle, always taking more, over and over as her tongue strokes and teases me.

It's too fucking much. This woman... I grip her hair tight and thrust into her throat. "Ready to swallow for me?"

She nods weakly and takes a sharp breath before letting me fuck her perfect mouth. She moans with me as wet, gasping sounds leave her throat with every thrust. I groan. "Yes, Abby. So ... fucking ...."

That's all I get out before I come. She digs her nails into my ass as I fill her throat. I draw back, making sure she can breathe. She sucks my cock again, making me groan.

By the time she lets me go, I'm shaking and panting, feeling like I need to cover myself since I'm so sensitive. Abby swallows, but doesn't move closer to me. I try to pull her against me, but she grabs my hand and lifts my arm, looking at my forearm.

"We need to fix this," she comments before swallowing again.

I roll on top of her and kiss her again and again until her hand softens on mine. She sighs, but when I draw back, she covers my mouth. "No more kisses until we fix your arm. I don't want you getting infected and I don't want you hurting after such a fun night."

Kissing her palm feels like the right answer.

She frees my mouth, and I grin. "Do you have a curling iron or something? We can burn it shut."

Horror contorts her face. "Danya!"

"I can call someone to come stitch me up," I offer. "Since you're not good with needles."

"We should keep this elevated and maybe do a tourni-quet. You're not bleeding as bad as I expected and then we should wrap it and clean it and-"

I kiss her cheek. "Ed and I did some basic first aid. It's not my first gunshot wound."

She narrows her eyes at me. I like that she's angry and not upset. She drags me to the bathroom, ignoring her nakedness since she's focused on grumbling about how little I care about myself. She looks at my arm, insists on washing it again, which is less than pleasant, and inspects it.

"Did you already burn the inside?" She asks.

"Yes," I grunt, still feeling the sizzle of the soap. "I wouldn't come back to you if I was close to dead."

She looks at her hair straightener, then back to me. "That will cause too big of a burn compared to the injury you have, so I'm going to wrap it."

"Okay," I accept.

She takes care of me, then swats my chest before ordering me to get in her bed.

I obey after she strips the comforter and top sheet. Abby grabs an oversized t-shirt that has dinosaurs on it, runs to the kitchen, and returns with ice and a glass of water. I feel my heart beat increase as she takes care of me.

She's a hell of a lot more than a pleasant view and a good lay.

FOURTEEN

Abby

DANYA FALLS ASLEEP AFTER I GET SOME FOOD AND WATER into him. I keep adjusting his ice, watching his bruise. I nibble at my lip. I'm tempted to call an old friend. He's a paramedic now, and he'd know if Danya's bruise is internal bleeding and a threat or just something I can treat. The internet hasn't been helpful.

I pace back and forth, playing with my phone. Would Sienna know?

As if someone in Danya's life can hear my thoughts, his phone buzzes. He left it on vibrate. I grab the phone and see "Lev". I pick it up. "Lev, how do you tell the difference between internal bleeding and a bruise?"

"Is it getting worse?" He asks.

"I ... I don't know. I've been applying ice, but bruises of this size tend to get worse before better," I answer. "I'm less worried about the bullet wound since it's not bleeding through the gauze, but the bruise could get worse."

"Idiot should have come in," he snorts. "Give me your address and I'll send someone over."

I glance down at myself, then at Danya. I'm washing his clothes, but they're still in the dryer. "Um ..."

"Internal bleeding isn't something to play around with," Lev hints.

"Fine, fine," I hiss. "Just ... send a good person."

I text him my address and set Danya's phone down. I run my fingers over his forehead, checking if he has a fever. He's a little warm, but not burning up. I touch his neck to get his pulse, remembering some of the basics I learned.

"You want more, Cupcake?" Danya asks.

"I want you to be okay," I respond.

He smiles as his eyes open. "I always am."

"Lev's sending someone over," I say. "Let me check your clothes."

He groans. "I didn't want anyone else to know where you lived."

"Edmon knows," I argue.

It takes another fifteen minutes for his clothes to dry, but Danya only accepts his underwear. He walks to my kitchen as if he's not damaged at all. I narrow my eyes. "Sit down and keep your arm elevated."

"You're cute," he says with a warm smile before kissing my temple. "Here, I thought you were all shy and sweet with the occasional sharpness."

I blush and look away.

"Then you show off how smart, strong, and biting you can be," he sighs, cupping my face between his hands. He kisses my forehead. "How dare you come around right when I swear off serious relationships."

Ah, that annoying little reminder. I suck my bottom lip. "Danya-"

Before I can tell him that our time is up, someone knocks on the door. He walks over to it after kissing me again. The large man that stood outside the bakery when Sienna and Lev came for a tasting stands there. He dips his head as he walks through the doorway.

"Karik, good to see you," Danya says.

They speak in Russian for a bit and Karik motions to another room. He inclines his head to me. "Miss Abby."

"Hi," I say.

Danya winks at me as he looks me over slowly. Karik shoves Danya into another room and I do the only thing I know how to do when stressed. I bake. Cookie dough is easy enough to make, and I put the sugar cookies in the oven, then make a frosting. I take a few deep breaths.

Now that someone else is taking care of Danya, there's room for panic in my head. He and his brother were covered in blood. Obviously, it wasn't all theirs and that means plenty of people are dead. Dead because of the man who just ...

I glance at my closed bedroom door and feel my face pale. I take a few deep breaths and focus on getting the right consistency for the frosting. It should be light and sweet.

The oven dings and I pull out the cookies, letting them cool on the pan so they have a satisfying crunch to the bottom.

I still need to wait to frost. I know better than to try to deal with hot cookies.

So, instead, I search my cupboards for the right sprinkles. I want the kind that looks like glitter. They're not as crunchy, better for the teeth, and they'll add a nice little extra something to the cookies.

"Cupcake." my shirt is jerked down, making me squeal. Danya continues to hold me. "I prefer you save that very sexy view for me alone."

"I can't reach the pink sprinkles," I insist, reaching for them anyway.

Danya gets them and puts them in my hand. "Am I allowed to steal a cookie?"

"Not yet. I have to frost them," I grumble.

He kisses my neck and wraps his arm around me,

palming my breast through the shirt. "I just got the all clear. Nothing life threatening, so I'd like to stay."

I drop the sprinkles. I look up at him, blink and shrug. "Is that okay with your brother? I don't want to upset ... him."

Danya bites my neck and pinches my nipple hard, making me yip and squirm. He groans as his other hand pulls at my shirt in the front, like he's going to finger me right here and now.

The large man says something in Russian, reminding me he's here. I push at Danya and he sighs before answering, his voice sharper than before.

They have a drawn out conversation as I frost the cooled cookies and put on some sprinkles. I package four cookies for the large man to take with him, then give him one on a napkin. He stops mid-sentence and stares at me.

"A cookie?"

"Thank you for coming so quickly," I say.

He looks from me to the cookie and takes a bite when Danya steals one. Danya chuckles. "Eat it Karik. This is Sienna's favorite baker."

Karik takes a bite and his eyes grow. He chews, swallows, then grins. "Delicious."

"Yes, she is," Danya purrs before nipping my earlobe.

"These are for Lev and Sienna. And Edmon, if he's still there. Whatever Danya doesn't eat, I'll send over too," I offer.

Karik offers me his hand. I shake his hand, but he turns my arm over. "No tattoos."

"I'm not that stupid," Danya huffs.

"You're a man. Makes you stupid enough," Karik says before continuing in Russian. He leaves quickly enough, leaving Danya and me alone ... again.

"Not ready to have me touch you in front of someone?" he asks, as if I'm a prude or something.

"It would have been rude. He was doing us a favor."

Danya chuckles and wraps himself around me from behind. "Was I too rough with you, Cupcake?"

"That should be my question," I answer, while turning in his arms to face him. "I should have waited to ask for that. You're all bruised and ... shot and ..."

"And I am capable of saying no if I don't want something," he assures me, his voice growing hard. "Don't start talking like you regret being with me."

"I don't."

"You sound like you do. Those orgasms don't mean a thing if you're having second thoughts now."

"I don't regret it, Daniel," I huff.

"Using my full name isn't very convincing."

I groan and shove by him, making sure to push on his chest and not his side. Danya follows me to the couch. I wrap a blanket around myself and take a few breaths. "You killed people."

"Da."

"And it doesn't bother you."

"No, it doesn't. This is my life, Abby. I kill people who need to be killed. They were happy to kill innocent people. They would have been happy to kill you, to kill my family, to do whatever it took to claim Miami as theirs. They're bad people."

"Why do you get to decide that?" I ask.

He sighs. "I follow orders. Lev has a softer heart now. He doesn't order us to kill without reason. One man put a hit on my brother's girlfriend."

"Danya-"

"I think you're more upset because you're not upset with how things turned out. You texted me when you felt unsafe earlier today. You knew, could feel that the man that sat down with you was a threat. You refused to go with him, you refused to drink what he gave you. Is that the kind of man you want walking around Miami, free and unbothered?" Danya challenges.

I hesitate.

"If you would have left with him, he would have held you hostage at best. He would have used you to get to us. You would have been some kind of bait and in their world, you don't need to be alive, in one piece, or happy to be bait," he says, leveling with me in every way.

His intense gaze is as cold and pissy as the first day I met him. Rather than staying back like most people would in a serious conversation, Danya moves closer to me and brushes my hair off my face, his fingers trailing across my chin.

"If this is too much for you, I'll try to understand that. I'll walk away and make it easy for you at Lev and Sienna's wedding. I think that would be a fucking waste, though," he says.

I look away from him. If I keep watching him, I won't want to let him go. There's something magical about Danya, something that makes me crave him even when I know I shouldn't. He likes my pissy side and accepts it. He praises my mild paranoia as smart. He loves my sweets, doesn't mind that I'm a workaholic as long as I enjoy it.

He's such a unique, amazing person, and that seems so much more important than the fact he just so happens to make a living killing people.

"Is murdering your job?" I ask.

"It's a part of it. Not the whole thing. I also protect business interests. I take care of getting things that we can't get. I'm just a very threatening delivery man. I handle some customer service style things–buying and selling–just with higher stakes," he answers.

"Don't you worry about selling things like that? Worrying about where they'll end up?" I whisper.

"If I'm worried about it, I don't sell it. I make Lev do it. Don't misunderstand–we are criminals, Abby. We're not some murderous Robin Hood characters. However, we're still people. I have a record from when I was young and stupid–trespassing, selling guns, drunk driving, the basics. I have some dangerous friends. I am a dangerous person."

"You've made that clear."

"But I'm not a threat to you. We've been seen together, so our connection is known to my world. I don't want that to scare you. Sienna and Lev have been together a long while. Lilah and Ed have been together. My father even has a girlfriend. It's getting more common for us mafia men to get civilian women," he says the last one with frustration.

"We agreed on a fake relationship. Just two weeks. Those two weeks were up about an hour after you left earlier. I know you don't do commitment, so where does that leave us now, Danya?" I ask.

He stares at me a long time, his eyes searching mine like I have the answer for him. I force myself to wait, to avoid filling in the answer. I want to know what Danya wants without giving him a clue as to what I want.

Aaron's not a problem anymore. So the only reason Danya should be with me now is because he wants to.

FIFTEEN

Danya

I SHOULD HAVE KNOWN THAT ABBY WAS KEEPING A TIMER. She's that kind of organized. Then again, we broke plenty of rules tonight. She got a glimpse of my life—something that I gave my brother's shit for in the past. I fucked her—breaking her most serious rule. And during all that, she made sure I was okay, made cookies, and is now having a serious conversation with me.

She's the strongest woman I've ever met. She reminds me of the Volkovs' wife. Where Valerie is sharp and threatening more often than not, Abby is sweet, observant, gentle and warm. She's kind and gives everyone a chance, even if it can bite her in the ass.

There's no way she *should* be able to survive in my world, but even knowing that, I can't imagine going home to my empty, cold home after meeting her. I want to be here, with her damn knickknacks, her sweets always available, her gentle smile, her blush, her laugh.

"I didn't realize it had already been two weeks," I mumble.

"It has."

"I'm not doubting you. You're the second most organized person I've ever met," I admit, running my hand through my hair. "I'm not convinced that Aaron-"

"Don't think of him. I'm not worried about him. Do you want to continue seeing me or ..." she takes a deep breath. "Or do you want to be done now?"

"Abby," I sigh.

"You said no commitment, but I won't keep sleeping with you if you're seeing someone else. I'm not saying that if we're done, we can't see each other. I enjoy spending time with you, so I'm happy to stay friends."

"Abby," I narrow my eyes.

"That's the first time I've said that to someone I've kissed and meant it. Huh," she looks at the ceiling a moment. "Anyway, I should have brought it up before we ended up ... tangled up in bed, but I don't regret sleeping with you."

"That wasn't 'sleeping together'," I growl. "It was fucking."

She blushes.

"And I didn't say I was ready to be done with you." I take her chin in my hand. "Stop trying to push me away."

"I don't know what else to do. I like you. Knowing what you do and what you're involved in doesn't change that. I didn't want to have feelings in this because it was supposed to be easy and now it's not," she murmurs.

"What in life is easy? Even reaching the sprinkles can be hard," I whisper.

She closes her eyes a moment and takes a breath. "So you want to continue in this gray area?"

"I won't see anyone else," I promise. "Beyond not having the time, I don't *want* to."

Abby's eyes open, and she studies my face. I lean forward, brushing my nose along hers. "I like how warm you are, how effortlessly happy you are. You're addictive."

She laughs and rubs my chest. "I'm not sleeping with you again tonight. You're too injured."

"That's a hell of a stipulation, cupcake," I growl.

"You'll survive. Now you have an incentive to survive, don't you?" she asks.

I roll my eyes and go get another cookie. I shove it into her hands and she laughs. We snack together, but I'm exhausted. I'm not sure I finish the cookie before the meds Karik gave me kick in.

I only wake up when I feel something move. I reach out, ready to defend myself, then open my eyes to find Abby trying to roll out of bed. She frees herself and kisses my temple. "Go back to sleep. You look exhausted."

I go back to sleep. Hours later, I get up and hear Abby humming to herself. I look at the time and shake my head. "You're supposed to be a at work."

"I took today off," she calls.

I stare out the doorway, shocked. I'm not sure Abby knows what a day off is, though. I walk into her living room and look her over. Those shorts are begging to be ripped off and that little tank top ... ugh, I want her naked again. Now.

"Do you know what a day off is?"

She turns to look at me and blushes. "I might have gone in for a little just to make sure there was enough to be open today."

"Mmhmm. How many hours?"

"Just ... three," she answers, biting her bottom lip. "The last thirty minutes was interviewing a potential new baker."

I close the space between us and rub her arms, kissing along her neck. "I'm proud of you."

"For considering three hours of work a day off?" she scoffs.

"For only staying three hours when you could have stayed a lot longer," I murmur. "I like your dedication to work."

She turns in my arms and kisses me, blushing and trying to shrink away. I tug on her pony, then kiss her, drawing it out, and moaning as I taste her and sugar. Lifting her onto the counter, I keep feasting on her mouth. I work on the button of her shorts and she gasps.

"Danya!"

"I told you I wasn't going to restrain myself anymore," I chuckle before biting her lip. I rub over the seam of her shorts, watching her tremble even as her thighs try and fail to close around my hand. "Anytime you're in a kitchen, I want to see if I can distract you."

"You're naughty," she grumbles. "I told you–no sex until you're not injured."

"Then don't fuck me. I can make you come without getting my cock involved," I growl before kissing her again.

Abby agrees and I prove myself again, eating her pussy until she can't focus on whatever she's baking. Once she's trying to push me away, saying it's too much, that I'm going to hurt her with my scruff, I feed her hungry kisses as I finger fuck her to one more orgasm.

She pants as she rests her head against my chest. "You're too much. Not allowed to come to the bakery anymore."

"We'll see about that."

"Danya-"

"I'll make sure to behave as long as there are customers," I barter.

She takes that win.

———

I HEAD HOME after a bit longer with Abby and spend the next day sleeping until I'm summoned to Lev's house. I drag myself in and my brother looks me over. "Well, you're alive."

"I am."

"The baker was worried about you," Lev informs me.

"Yeah. Karik showing up was a surprise," I admit.

Lev watches me, and I notice the smirk playing on his lips. I roll my eyes. "Don't start gloating."

"Weren't you going to push away relationships and be devoted to the mafia?" Lev asks.

"I'm not in love with her. She's just good for me right now. Why end it with her when the wedding is coming up?" I ask, trying to minimize everything.

What I feel for Abby is between us alone. I'm not ashamed of her, nothing like that. I'm more ashamed of myself. I'm supposed to be lethal, intimidating, charming when I want to be, but married to the Mafia. I should be what my brothers aren't–devoted. They have distractions and that means I have to be the one to keep them alive.

Lev smirks and tries to hide it behind his palm. "Sure, sure you are."

"Any updates from our sisters?" I ask, trying to distract him.

Of course it works. Lev can't talk enough about Ana and how well she's doing in college. Our older sister has always been independent. She's been in Russia the last few years, disconnected from our family. Lev's frustrated he has heard nothing on if she'll be coming to his wedding. He reached out to family in Russia, but still has heard nothing.

Now that he's distracted, I give my report about what Ed and I took care of. Misha's not a problem. We took care of the cartel, reaffirming the lines drawn in Miami and proved we're a strong chapter of the mafia, one that shouldn't be taken lightly.

Lev lets me go after that, telling me to get better. I text Abby every day, call her every night, but keep my promise to focus on healing and getting better. I sleep plenty between sending orders and making sure our businesses have what they need.

After four full days, I can't stand it anymore and based on Abby asking how I'm doing more and more often, her questions on if I'll be coming over today, if I need her to bring me dinner, I know she wants to see me too. I grin as I pull on jeans and a t-shirt, happy to show off my tattoos. I look at my arm, it's healing well, so I take off the gauze and let it breathe today. I'll have to cover it with tattoos once it heals enough. There's a reason I have so many. People accept tattoos a lot more than they accept these kind of scars.

Not that it stops me from showing up at the bakery. For the first time, I look up at the name of the shop: Sweet Escape.

I chuckle to myself as I walk in and happen upon Aaron. I narrow my eyes and Mona notices me. She motions from me to Aaron as Aaron lays into Abby. "I told you he'd leave. I notice shit. So how about you suck up your pride and come back to where you belong? That guy was out of your league."

Mona laughs. "I'd choose my words carefully if I were you, asshole."

"Shut it," he orders, then reaches across the counter. I hear a smack and he groans. "What the fuck!"

"Don't touch me. I'm not yours. I'm not coming back to you. I don't care if I'm dumped. I don't care if I end up alone with only cupcakes and the stray cats I feed. All of that is better than being with you. Go, have fun with the girls that took care of you when I didn't. I'm done accepting the scraps of your kindness." Abby's voice is stronger, more demanding than I've ever heard.

"I'm a nice guy and you're just like-"

"People who are *actually* nice don't have to say it," Abby snarls.

Rather than confronting Aaron and tossing him out of the bakery, I walk around the back and rub the back of Abby's neck. "What did I miss, Cupcake?"

"You," Aaron points at me. "You messed her up."

"How did I do that?" I snort. "Maybe you were the one stifling her."

"You're banned from my shop," Abby points at Aaron. "Come back in and I will call the police. Continue harassing me and I'll get a restraining order to make sure you can't keep popping back up in my life."

Aaron looks between us, his face going purple, then he storms out of the bakery, slamming the door behind him. Mona hums to herself as she adjusts the pastries. Abby drags me back to the kitchen, then hugs me. "I'm happy to see you."

"I'm happy to see you standing up to that asshole," I agree, kissing her hungrily. "My bruise is all yellow."

She looks at my arm, then pulls out a first aid kit and puts neon band-aids on the entry and exit wounds. After that, she nods. "Then you're in good enough shape."

I arch an eyebrow.

"Mona's got headphones in," Abby explains.

I groan and kiss her, backing her against the table. "Please tell me you have some frosting made."

"Kinky," she pants against my lips. "Of course I do."

"Fucking hell, woman. You're going to destroy my control," I moan as I rip her button up, determined to have Abby every single way I need her right now.

SIXTEEN

Abby

DANYA NAKED IN MY KITCHEN AT WORK IS SOMETHING I never thought I'd see. He has me on my table as he fucks me grinding and slamming into me, making me moan until all I can do is hold on to him. He licks his favorite frosting off my breasts, sucking and licking until my body is on fire with need.

"Fuck, we should have done this with a shower close by," he groans.

"I don't care," I pant, lifting his chin to kiss him.

Danya groans and moves his tongue with mine as he pushes my thighs wider and pounds deeper into me. My head falls back as I hold on to his shoulder, digging my nails in to him as I roll my hips with his.

His lips slip around my nipple, sucking and licking until my whole body trembles. He pushes me back so I'm lying on my own table, then rubs my clit as he continues eating frosting off me.

I can't take it. He feels too good, knows just how to please me, ruins every other sexual experience I've ever had with his willingness to do everything, try everything.

"Danya!" I whine.

"You're a whole fucking meal, Cupcake. My gorgeous. *Zhizn moya,*" he snarls, dissolving into Russian.

"Harder," I beg. "Fuck me harder, Danya!"

He grabs my throat and holds me down, leaning over me so I can see the heat in his gaze, the pleasure written on his gorgeous face. I stroke down his abs, loving how his body moves under my touch and he fucks me so hard my table is forced against the wall over and over again.

I don't even care if customers hear. Nothing matters but Danya, staring at me like I'm the only woman in the world he wants, like I'm the only person he could ever want to be with.

"Mine," he snarls before biting my breast.

A whine leaves my throat, but he does it again and again. I'm so close to the edge, dangling on it, desperate to fall over and into the ecstasy he can give.

"Fucking ... come!" He orders, squeezing the sides of my throat as he lifts my leg over his shoulder and swats my ass hard. "Come or I'll have to try something new."

New sounds so good, especially considering this new angle has him rubbing against my clit every time he fills me. My eyes roll back and my back arches on the table. He licks over my other nipple–still covered in frosting and groans with me.

His fingers move from my butt cheek along my crack and to my backdoor. I jump as he circles there, but the second he pushes down, I come apart. My voice breaks, so my mouth hangs open silently as my core tightens around Danya's cock.

My legs twitch as I squirm and writhe under him, trying to pull him closer and push him away at the same time. Danya's growl fills my ear as my whole body burns away, leaving me with nothing but pleasure itself, total and complete bliss.

"*Zhizn moya,*" he growls as I come to, my eyes opening

slowly, my body limp and languid. I can barely think, can barely move as he releases my throat and guides me off my table and onto my knees. "Finish me."

I grab the back of his thighs and eagerly suck his cock, taking him as deeply as I can down my throat. He tastes like me and his own salty flavor. I moan and close my eyes, but he grips my chin, keeping me from moving on him.

"Eyes on me, only me," he commands, his voice low and husky.

I meet his intense, dark gaze and open my mouth wider to fit more of him down my throat. He groans and his jaw tightens, his eyes dilate, and his hand slides back into my hair to guide me over his cock.

Danya moves me like he needs, takes control even though blow jobs are supposed to be something I do myself. I love it all the same. I love how he owns what he likes, how he teaches me what to do, and we both enjoy the process.

"Fuck, your mouth is so damn good," he snarls.

I moan around him and he shudders before tugging my hair hard. "Take me as deep as you can and suck hard, Abby. Give me everything, so I'll come for you."

That's all the encouragement I need. I jerk him closer to me and force him as far down my throat as I can. I use a trick I learned from a Cosmo blog to help with my gag reflex, even though my throat threatens to close around him entirely.

I make a sound I'm less than proud of, some kind of wet sucking sound combined with a whine, and Danya's hand tightens in my hair to the point of pain before he comes down my throat.

He groans as his legs shake for me. I stroke up his abs as I slowly release his cock, licking along his length. His abs tighten against my hands and he sighs when I pop off the head of his dick.

"Fuck, *Zhizn moya*," he rasps, pulling me up off my knees and kissing me hungrily.

Danya backs me against the table behind me like we're going to go for round two. He cups the back of my neck and continues kissing me, ignoring the fact that whatever's left of the frosting we used is getting all over both of us.

Even as Danya pulls my underwear back on me and wipes my chest off with a towel, he keeps kissing me.

"We're going to have a lot of fun, Abby," he promises me.

I giggle and lick some frosting off his chest. He chuckles. "Like your own frosting?"

"I like it on you even more," I say.

He groans and lifts my chin to bite my bottom lip. "Stop tempting me into another round."

Danya and I clean each other up as much as possible, then get dressed. I insist on teaching him how to make frosting, since we need more if I'm going to manage today. But he pulls me into the circle of his arms and kisses my temple.

"Hi, is Danya here?" A voice asks. "Hello? I'm sorry, I'm just ..."

"Oh, hi! I'm sorry," Mona answers.

Danya's frozen against me though, one arm wrapped around me as his other brushes his hip. I grab that hand. "Hey, we talked about you bringing guns here."

"And you know exactly who and what I am," he reminds in my ear. "Doesn't that make you hotter for me?"

I rub my ass against him until he groans and his hand tightens on my shirt. "If you don't stop teasing me, I'm going to have to drag you out of here and show you what your teasing earns you."

Giggling, I shake my head and stand on my toes to kiss his jaw. "But someone's here for you."

"Don't care," he croons, his hand stroking down until he's bunching my dress up. "I'm not here. I'm with you."

The fact that he's so turned on by me, the fact that he's so determined to have me - it blows my mind. Even at my best with Aaron, he was done after one round and ready to move on to the next thing. None of my boyfriends have baked with me, especially not *after* sex.

Danya's the first person to insist on being around me so much, with or without sex. Turning in his arms, I wrap my arms around his neck and kiss him slowly. Danya moans and strokes my cheek gently.

When he releases me, we stare at one another and I suck my bottom lip to avoid saying something cheesy or too sweet.

"Hey, you two done?" Mona asks.

Danya grins, still only looking at me. "With the fun stuff ... for now."

"Good, because there's someone at the counter for you," Mona points at him, but her tone and face aren't pleasant. "A girl."

"Is it Sienna? I have the mock up for her cake almost done, I just need another half hour and-"

"No, Abby, not Sienna." Mona narrows her eyes at Danya. "Have something to say, Danny?"

Danya shrugs and takes my hand, leading me out from the back as if I'm the guest and he's the owner. Still, the fact he doesn't want to let me go and that he's eager to be with me, to show me off even, makes my heart beat double time.

A girl with dark hair up in a pony wearing clothes that make her look like a teacher. She's shorter than me, thin, pretty. She looks at Danya with sharp eyes, sharper eyes than I expect from her from knowing her all of five seconds.

"Danya, we need to talk."

"What did Ed do now?" Danya asks, rubbing my hand with his thumb. "If this is another fight-"

"It's not a fight. He was called to business in the middle of a date, so it's obviously important and I'm confused about why you're *not* there. He said things were fine after the last bit of business a few days ago," she says while looking around. "Tell me what's going on."

"If I knew, I would, Lilah."

"Well! Find out!"

Danya sighs. "Give me a second." He pauses instead of heading to the back, then turns around to face me. "Lilah, this is my ... my Abby. Abby, this is Ed's girlfriend."

Lilah rolls her eyes as Danya heads away. Mona shrugs and motions for us to go sit down. I grab a peach and cream cupcake and a classic vanilla and lead Lilah over to a table. She sighs as she sits down.

"I know that Edmon is plenty capable. He always comes home, but sometimes it gets to me. Normally, it's kind of hot that he does what he does and it doesn't.. it's not a problem, but sometimes I hate it."

"Want a cupcake?"

She moans and takes the vanilla. I smile and take the peach. Her leg keeps bouncing. "Edmon and I have been through so much. Honestly, I think it's therapy worthy, but even in the worst of it, I trust him to stay alive. It's one of the many things he's good at... it might be the thing he's best at, which is saying something, but it worries me too."

"I can understand that," I admit.

"Really?"

"I met Danya at the engagement party when I saw plenty of things I didn't want to see," I admit.

"You were caught up in that?" She gasps, then reaches across the table to take my hand. "I'm so sorry."

"And then he got the call about ... business while we were together and he ran off, telling me to defend myself and came back covered in blood," I whisper.

She nods and squeezes my hand. "But you're still with him?"

"Yeah. It actually doesn't bother me like it should. I

guess I got all the shock out that first night. I don't know. Things are kind of easy with Danya in a lot of ways," I admit.

"And he called you his."

I roll my eyes.

"You'll get used to it. The twins have this vendetta against anything that takes them away from the Mafia or distracts them from what they consider their job and life," she assures me. "But trust me, I haven't seen Danya light up like this with anyone or put any business to the side. You're special to him."

I feel like I'm glowing hearing that, but at the same time, I remember his warning about that being dangerous and I'm not sure if it's a good or bad thing to continue this relationship.

SEVENTEEN

Danya

"WHAT'S GOING ON, ED?" I DEMAND IN RUSSIAN. "YOUR girlfriend is here demanding answers."

"I was just called in because the clean-up crew's number doesn't match ours. There's one missing. One was alive," Ed reports.

"And which *one* was that?" I growl.

"The one that you added to the damn list!" He hisses. "Julio, whatever. The one that you said was a problem because of Abby. Either you weren't thorough, or he was revived."

I close my eyes tightly and grit my teeth. "He got away?"

"Don't use that tone with me. That was your solo job. You fucked it up, you can fix it," he snarls. "We're getting info. Keep Lilah there. She's safe with you."

"I'm the one who gets to take him out."

"Sure, whatever. I just want this done."

Ed hangs up on me and I return to the girls. I look between them as Lilah arches an eyebrow. Abby looks at me and offers me half her cupcake. I take an appreciative bite and sit down with them.

"He's fine. The unfinished business concerns Abby and

me. Right now, we just need to stay together," I inform them.

Abby looks at me, licking the frosting from her top lip and I groan. I want her right now. It doesn't matter that we just had sex, seeing her with frosting has my stomach tightening. She shoves me. "Don't look at me like that. There are three of us, not two."

Lilah bits her bottom lip. "Edmon's not in danger, right?"

"No, he's fine," I assure her, reaching under the table to rub Abby's thigh.

"I'm sure he's in better shape than whoever's in trouble," Abby says. "And until you're ready, you can eat as many cupcakes as you want. You can enjoy them all."

"Well, your vanilla is really good," Lilah mumbles. "Maybe I could have a small cake, more than a cupcake, and some coffee."

"Coming right up," Abby jumps up to take care of it.

Lilah arches her eyebrow at me. "Seems like you like her."

"Don't start, Lilah," I warn her.

"It starts out small. You like kissing her. You like fucking her. Then you end up liking her and then you end up *loving* her."

I don't like that chain of events at all. That's how Ed fell to Lilah. Lev fell even faster. I'm pretty sure he fell in love with Sienna when we were kids, before he ever kissed her, fucked her, did anything. And now ...

I look over at Abby as she hums and pulls out a cake for Lilah. I remember her sharpness and see that same look in her eyes when she looks at me. She knows exactly who's in trouble and I can tell that if that man walks into her shop, she'll make him pay for coming back from the dead.

"I do like her," I admit. "A lot. I still have plenty to figure out, though, so don't-"

"Oh, she already knows," Lilah says confidently. "She wouldn't put up with you if she didn't like you."

"Well, I am a pretty good ex-boyfriend repellent. I could make that a job and rent out my services," I say, cocky and with an easy smile.

Lilah just shakes her head at me. "Oh stop. You wouldn't rent out boyfriend duties when you want to be her boyfriend."

I flip her off while scratching my face, and she leans across the table to swat at me. Abby sets the cake down and sits next to me, but I pull her onto my lap. She stares up at me. "Don't you remember what I said about PDA?"

"Is this too much? After what we just did in-"

She puts her hand over my mouth, her face burning red. "You stop that."

I kiss her palm and lean into her hand. Abby huffs. "I'm too heavy to be on top of you."

"You're not too heavy," I insist, giving Lilah a look. She shakes her head at me. I look between them. "What? Trust me, *Zhizn moya*, I can take care of plenty if you let me." I pull her hand off my face and press my lips to her ear. "I can put you in all kinds of positions, Cupcake."

She blushes deeper and Lilah laughs softly. "Told you so, Danya."

I roll my eyes at her. After an hour, Lilah is restless. She groans. "Can't we just go to my place? There are two rooms, so you guys can capitalize on all this tension and I can be comfortable at home."

Abby's been working nonstop for the last forty-five minutes. I motion to her and Lilah groans. "I should be at work, but Ed left lunch so suddenly, I took the rest of the day. I don't want my students in danger and I know that where I work is publicized, so ..."

"I get it. She's a workaholic, though. And she looks so

good working, doesn't she?" I ask, shamelessly gushing over her. "She's so determined and sweet."

Lilah shakes her head. "You've got it bad."

"If someone comes into the shop and she's not here to defend it, I'll be afraid of her," I admit.

"Really? Her?"

Abby gives a smile even when a customer yells at her for putting peanuts in a peanut turtle cupcake. Abby handles it gently, sweetly, and I look back at Lilah. "Trust me, there's plenty to be afraid of there."

"I'm sure she could shame you with her endless patience and a pout," Lilah teases.

Abby finishes up with the customer and returns to me. "I'm so over customers not reading. It literally says 'peanuts'. Why couldn't she avoid it if her son has an allergy?"

Lilah arches an eyebrow. "Why didn't you tell her that?"

"My business is my baby. If I let every customer who upset me get their way or if I lost my temper with each customer, then I wouldn't have as many customers that return. Plus, sometimes, if customers see one customer being rude, they buy more. But don't tell anyone that. It's a business secret."

Lilah laughs at Abby and Abby looks at me sucking her bottom lip.

"Do we need more frosting?" I ask in a low voice.

She shoves me. "Stop it."

"You know, Abby. Your shop is only open for another hour and there are plenty of sweets, so how about we get out of here?"

"Sure ... this is our slow time anyway," she looks around, then Abby darts away. She grabs Mona and I follow with my gaze.

"Yeah, she had a good gut instinct," Lilah says to me, even though she's not looking at me.

I turn and see the man that was sitting with Abby. Julio. I narrow my eyes at him. He looks at me and pulls a gun.

"You try to kill me for what? Because I'm a better man for her?"

"Please. You wouldn't know what to do with Abby. You'd fall all over yourself," I snarl.

"You don't get it. She's a pawn," he snorts. "I'm sure she is for you, too. She's a way for you to stay busy and appear normal. She's a way to keep you in a spot I can find you."

He looks like shit. He's bruised, kind of bloody, really messed up in general. I definitely did a number on him. I get up, but he cocks the gun. "Move. I'd love to take out one of your family."

Lilah starts to move, but he turns the gun on her. I edge in front of her. My brother would never forgive me if I let something happen to her. I know if I reach for my own gun, I'll lose some blood or my life and I won't be able to help anyone.

Taking a breath, I stare at Julio. "What's the vendetta?"

"What are you talking about?" he demands.

At the same time, Abby pops up from behind the counter, holding a cast iron skillet. I have no idea what she uses it for, but I'm glad she has it. She keeps creeping up behind him, so I focus on keeping his attention.

"There's always a vendetta, isn't there?" I ask. "Always someone thinking they're noble and fighting the good fight again and again, always thinking that they're doing the right thing or avenging people that are already dead."

He scoffs. "You don't know me."

"I know everyone who comes up against my family. They're either terrible or they just want to believe they're doing the right thing a little too late. It's alright. It might be noble, but is dying really worth it? You could have run off and lived a full life." I shrug. "I guess you'd rather be dead."

"The second you reach for that gun, it's all over. You

should know that. You can't beat me, not like this," he laughs.

Lilah gasps and grabs my shoulder. Just as Julio lifts his hand, gun pointed directly at me, Abby brings the cast iron down on his arm, then brings it back against his head. He drops to the ground, either dead or close to it.

Abby drops the skillet, then kicks him. I run to her and pull her back so she doesn't keep fighting him.

"Lilah, call the police please," I request.

"Done," Lilah answers.

Abby keeps fighting. "No, he threatened my shop! He threatened Lilah, he threatened me, and he threatened you! I need to hit him again!"

"Easy, *Zhizn moya*. Let's not have your first kill be so public," I say in her ear.

"He deserves it! He tried to kill you! You!"

I hold her close to me and keep petting her hair, trying to calm her down as she continues telling me how much she needs to fight him, to make him pay, to do a lot worse than she's already done. Her spiteful, vicious self has me so turned on, I don't want to wait for the police.

Eventually they come and we talk it out, so we give statements and he's taken first to the hospital, but with the promise of jail in the air. Lilah runs off right away and Mona sighs. "Guess the shop is going to be closed tomorrow?"

"No!" Abby groans. "No, I can't let him win!"

"Hey," I turn her chin to me. "You have a day off."

"Yeah?"

"And that means I can make plans with you."

She stares at me, lips parted. "But ... but work?"

"Teach me some recipes or we can come up with our own." I pull her tighter against me. "Or I can teach you how to fight."

"I'm pretty handy with a cast iron," she mumbles. "I might need a new one after denting it on his face, though."

"Shopping, baking, fighting ... it all sounds like foreplay to me," I tease with a wink.

Abby gasps and shoves me. "Danya! You can't say things like that in public."

"Then you better take me out of public, Cupcake. I want to do a lot more than 'say things'."

She takes my hand and tries to drag me out back, but I turn and pull her to my car. "I'm not getting on your vespa."

"It's totally safe!"

"It won't carry both of us, and I'm not about to waste time when I want you ... now," I insist.

She moans and gets in the car just to start moaning again since I can't keep my hands to myself. She complains about someone seeing, but doesn't push me away, doesn't tell me no, and when I stop before she can come, she gives me a vicious look, puts her fingers over mine and shows me exactly how she likes to be touched.

This is the side of Abby I just might love.

EIGHTEEN

Abby

AFTER A ROUND AND A HALF OF SEX AT MY PLACE (ONLY HALF because shower sex doesn't work well and only using our hands doesn't feel like it counts), Danya and I cuddle on my couch. I have on his shirt, which means he's just in boxers, all his tattoos exposed. Anytime he looks at me he groans and kisses me, even if I have my mouth full of the Chinese food we ordered.

"Danya!" I complain after swallowing. "You're going to make me choke on the noodles."

He chuckles and pulls me closer. "I have a break and you have a break. Let's see if we can tolerate each other overnight, da?"

"That's something reserved for boyfriends," I grumble.

I'm still not entirely sure where we stand on that. He introduced me to Lilah as 'his' Abby, but not as his girl-friend. I feel like we're still up in the air. Granted, I was ready to kill just because someone had a gun pointed at him ... then again I think I would have done that if there was a gun pointed at Mona or Lilah too.. and I just met Lilah.

"So being willing to take a bullet for you doesn't earn me that title?"

"We were fake dating for two weeks."

"What about it was fake, really?"

"You tell me!" I stand up and cross my arms over my chest. "I'm serious. I told you from the beginning, the mafia thing doesn't bother me. I can obviously handle your sass and constant come-ons. I can handle a lot, but you don't want commitment. You said we'd try it out, but that doesn't mean labels are involved and I don't want to ..."

Danya cocks his head to the side even though his eyes travel the length of me. He sighs and spreads his arms over the back of the couch. "You don't want to what, Cupcake?"

"You're smart, you fill in the blank," I grumble.

"There's plenty I'd like to fill," he answers before reaching for the hem of his shirt where it rests on my thighs.

I swat at his hand. "Can we have a conversation where you're not flirting with me?"

His smile melts. Cold Danya is back, the calculating gaze, the way his lips twitch slightly down, his expression in general makes me feel like I've disappointed him, which is definitely not the goal, but I stand my ground.

"I can't fill in the blank, Abby. You haven't given me enough information. What don't you want to do?"

I take a slow breath.

"You don't want to be with me?"

"No, I obviously do," I argue.

He moves closer. "You don't want me to touch you at all in public?"

"I'm ... trying to get used to that, that's not-"

"Then what?" He stands up, towering over me. "That's what my 'smarts' come up with when you give me half sentences and hide things from me."

"I'm not hiding things!" I exclaim. "I'm just not saying things. It's different."

He arches an eyebrow, crossing his thick arms over his chest. The silence stretches until I can't stand it. I'm uncomfortable and the way he's staring at me makes me feel wrong and off.

"I don't want you to leave because I get too boring or because I'm too much or ..."

"You're not too much."

"You've known me for three weeks, Daniel. That's barely anything."

"Which is why I want to spend the night. I want to get to know you. How can you give me a title if you don't know me and I don't know you, huh?"

"I don't even know why you want the title. You said you didn't want commitment and a title pretty much cements that," I grumble, stumbling a step back. "Look, it's not that I don't like you. I do. You make me feel amazing, but ..."

"Issues with the ex?"

"No, issues with me. I can't put myself through what I went through with Aaron again. I can't give my heart to someone who only wants me for sex or who only wants me when things are easy. You've gotten to be the hero over and over again, will I be enough for you without the excitement?"

"*You* are plenty exciting, Abigail," he whispers, unfolding his arms and taking my hands. "I like being here with you. My whole life is drama and murder and intensity. I love it, I do, but I also like these easy moments with you. I like holding you in my arms and at least being half sure you're not planning on stabbing me. I like baking with you. I like that you're not afraid of me. I like *this*," he insists, then drops my hands to take my face between his palms. "I like *you*."

My body trembles as I watch him. I don't want to believe it mostly because it's exactly what I want to hear. But Danya doesn't say things to pad my ego or to make things easier. He never has. He's never given me a reason to question if he's lying and he's obviously never lied about his compliments or flirting, considering what we just spent the last two hours doing.

"You want to try this ... really?" I ask.

"I know you do too," he murmurs. "You beat a man for threatening your business and people you care about. You yelled at someone who took a tip and was willing to drug you even though you were drunk. You don't cower away from anything now, not even your ex."

"I'm scared of spiders," I admit, my nose wrinkling. "I don't like bugs at all."

"We'll have to hire someone to take care of spiders. I'm not fond of them either. When my brother got that damn spider tattoo, I refused to stand on that side of him unless it was covered," he admits.

"You're a killer and you're afraid of spiders?"

"They have too many legs and they bite and if we keep talking about them, I'm going to be convinced that there are spiders around." he glances around, then pulls me against him. "I'm good to protect you against lizards."

"I like lizards."

Somehow, we end up talking about what we're afraid of. When I bring up clowns, Danya nods. "That's not fear. That's common sense. It's a proper thing to be afraid of. What are they hiding under that makeup?"

"And the shoes!" I agree.

He grins and cuddles me close again. "I'll protect you from clowns and horror movies. We'll figure out how to deal with spiders and rats."

"I can handle rats. I used to have them as pets when I was a kid," I say.

He unwraps his arms from around me. "And we're done here."

I shove him back and he chuckles, pulling me into a kiss. "I knew you wanted me, Cupcake."

"What do you keep calling me in Russian?" I ask as I play with his fingers.

He hesitates and blushes. I think it's the first time he's ever looked embarrassed around me. He clears his throat. "It just … it just slips out sometimes. It's …"

"There has to be some translation you can give me," I insist.

"It's a pet name, that's all."

"Are you going to teach me Russian?"

"Learn it by kissing me long enough. Then you'll be able to make your mouth into the shapes you'll need," he purrs.

I can't resist. I press my lips to his and Danya kisses me slowly. He steadily lies me back onto the couch, stroking through my hair, then pulling my thighs around him. He makes me feel small, feminine, perfect. He licks into my mouth and lets out a slow groan.

Danya draws out every moment, like he wants to take his time and memorize the way we move together, how we feel. When he strays from my mouth, he kisses along my jaw, making me pant, then continues along my throat.

"Danya …" I moan.

"Do you want me to stop?"

"No. I don't want to stop," I insist.

"Have you had enough of me?"

"No," I answer, my lips brushing his again. "You should spend the night … or stay until you annoy me."

He chuckles and nips my bottom lip. "I want to fuck you against the window so you can watch the city move as I bury myself inside you."

I nod against him. "Yes."

"You'll be completely naked. Anyone with a telescope-"

"Then we should hope someone's watching with a telescope, shouldn't we?" I ask as I lift my hips against his.

Danya groans and shakes his head. "The last thing

anyone would call you is boring, Cupcake. And if they do call you that, they're wrong."

We follow through on his plan. He picks me up, walks me to the floor-to-ceiling windows, then strips me naked. I pull on his boxers until he pushes me back against the window and kisses down my body, pulling my leg over his shoulder to bury his face between my legs.

I gasp and press one palm to the chilly window and hold on to Danya's head with the other until I come apart, shaking and whimpering. My head falls back against the glass and Danya draws back, staring up at me with his lips all shiny.

"Be careful. I like your head, don't hurt it," he says as he stands.

I pull him close and kiss up his neck and stand on my toes to bite his ear. "Fuck me."

He groans and spins me around, spanking me hard. "Curse *more*."

Danya presses my body against the window and slams into me. I moan and pant against the window, fogging it up with every breathy moan. "Danya!"

"Imagine someone looking up here, seeing you moaning as I fuck you hard. I want them to see you, to hear you, to know that only I can make you come like this, can make you so wild," he growls in my ear.

I'm hoping for it right away. I want to be seen, want people to be jealous of me or Danya, either both, and to enjoy the view knowing that they are only getting a fraction of the pleasure. It takes me an embarrassingly short time to come for him, but he doesn't stop, he just jerks my hips further back, so I'm bent over, holding onto the window sill to stay standing as Danya slams into me over and over again.

"Please!" I moan.

"You want me to fuck you harder?"

"Touch my … Ugh, do it like in the bakery," I say, unable to force the words out.

"Dirty girl, aren't you?" He snarls, but his finger teases my ass again. He works it in and my whole body heats. It's wrong, taboo, terrible in so many ways, but I like it. I like that he's willing to push boundaries, try new things, and reward me with pleasure. "*Zhizn moya!*"

"Yes! Fuck me hard!" I beg.

Danya pushes us both over the edge, his finger buried in my ass, his cock buried so deeply inside me that I'm sure I'll feel him forever. He barely jerks out in time, coming on my inner thigh as he holds onto me.

"Such a good girl for me," he purrs.

"Only for you," I say, breathlessly.

Danya gets me through another shower, then we lie in bed together. He glances under it and I swat at him. "There are no spiders."

"I was checking for clowns," he teases.

I curl against him and huff. "Now I'm going to have nightmares about them."

"My gun is on the bedside table. I'll take care of any clown that comes in here and tomorrow, I'll teach you how to do the same," he promises before yawning. "Goodnight, Cupcake."

"Night, stud," I hum.

He chuckles and kisses the top of my head, rubbing my back as I lie on his chest. I could get used to this.

NINETEEN

Danya

OVER THE NEXT FEW WEEKS, WORKING AND NOT, I SPEND more time with Abby. She takes to firing guns and enjoys it. Three weeks after we agree to committing ourselves to each other–in our own way, I decide to take Abby somewhere special, somewhere I haven't taken anyone or gone on my own.

It's a place within our territory, but a place I never went. I didn't want to take the risk of getting hurt, plus who has time to ride mini rollercoasters and rides on a pier. There was never any reason to spend time there when I could be patrolling and taking care of the mafia business.

Luckily, we're in a lull–other chapters aren't bothering us and the cartel is behaving so why not take advantage of that and treat Abby to something now that she's taking weekends off and trying not to work more than ten hours a day?

I show up at her door Saturday evening and knock twice. She opens the door wearing shorts and a cute top that ties under her tits, revealing plenty of cleavage. If there's a Ferris Wheel, I can't be sure I won't pay someone to leave it for ten minutes so I can take advantage of her outfit.

"You should wear skirts more," I hum, not sure if I'm talking to Abby or myself.

"Hmm?" she asks as she locks the door.

I jerk her against me and kiss her, dragging it out until she fists my shirt in her hand. It's my favorite response. Like she can't get enough, doesn't want to miss out on a thing. I nip her bottom lip and press her back against the wall. She rubs my sides and I draw back, giving her a naughty smile.

"I bet we could get away with some naughty stuff right here," I tease in her ear. "Who needs a date when we can do that?"

She giggles, her eyes squinting. "You're determined to make all my neighbors hate me, aren't you?"

"Oh? Is that what I'm doing or is that just a consequence of making you come every single time I'm with you?" I ask.

She blushes and shoves at me. "You're so terrible."

"Then I'll stop with the orgasms. Got it."

"No! I just mean-"

"Either you're fishing for me to use ball gags or you're going to use your neighbors hating you as an excuse to move in with me," I chuckle as I lead her down the stairs. "It's not the worst reason."

Abby doesn't sass me or answer until we're standing by my car. She's staring at me with her lips parted. We stare at each other and I clear my throat. "What is it?"

"You want me to move in with you?"

"I was ..." Was I joking? I feel like I've started saying more than I mean when it comes to Abby. Like I can't control what comes out of my mouth when I'm around her. I clear my throat and squeeze her wrist. "Maybe?"

"Oh," she breathes.

I open the car door for her and she slides in. When she doesn't reach for the seatbelt, I reach in and pull it across her chest, letting my fingers trail over her cleavage. "Does that scare you, cupcake?"

"Maybe," she breathes.

I shut the door, trying not to slam it since she's mentioned she doesn't like that. I get in and put the key in the car, but pause before pulling out. "You know where I keep my gun and my knife at all times. I know where you keep your "swinging skillet". We're celebrating your birthday tonight. We've been together for over a month … how long do couples wait before they move in?"

Abby shrugs. "I don't know. Aaron kind of moved in because his lease with his last roommate was up and then I left him and paid to break the lease before moving into my place. I do need to resign in a month."

I let that sizzle between us on the way to the pier. When I park, I walk around to open the door, but jump out of the way before Abby hits me with it. I snort. "You never let me be a gentleman."

"You are one without opening doors," she says as if it's simple. "Give me time to think about the moving in question?"

"Sure, it was one of those thoughts that got a little too serious too fast, so there's no pressure," I answer with an easy smile.

"I bet your place is spider free, though," she teases me.

I narrow my eyes at her. "We're not reliving that."

"Considering you had to replace my alarm clock because you threw it at the spider, I agree," she squeezes my hand. "What are we doing here?"

"You're a closeted thrill seeker, so I decided to see how much of a thrill you can handle," I motion to the lit up pier. "There's plenty of food, too."

Her eyes sparkle, catching the light, and she moves closer to me. "I haven't been here since I was fourteen!"

With that, she drags me to the pier. I let Abby show off

her excitement, dragging me from place to place, until she pauses and bites her lip, looking up at me. "I'm being too much, aren't I?"

"You're never too much, *Zhizn moya*," I promise, kissing her temple. "It's a date. If you weren't this excited, I'd worry that I didn't choose a good option for us."

She stands on her toes and kisses me, holding me in place as she teases me with her tongue. "Good, because I'm going to kick your butt in Skee-ball."

"Sure you are," I wink.

Abby does kick my ass ruthlessly. She bounces and giggles, but we keep playing arcade games, piling tickets together until I can buy some silly mood ring that would have been cheaper to get online. I pocket it, since Abby's already run off.

If I hadn't insisted that she keep a taser in her purse, I'd be frustrated with her. I might be over protective after everything, but I don't care much about that. I'm in the Mafia, she knows that, and she knows that people have seen us together.

How silly of me to think that wasn't a kind of commitment back when it first happened. We end up on a few rides, sharing cotton candy even though I hate how sticky it is and how overly-sweet it tastes.

It's an amazing night. Even just walking around with other normal couples and people would be more than enough with Abby. She leans against me, rubbing my belly. "Are you sure you're feeling okay after the scrambler?"

"My stomach is made of steel. It doesn't matter how nauseous I get," I say with pride.

"Sure," she pats my stomach until I wince. "So you want to go find some fried food to eat?"

"I'd rather kiss you or ..."

Her cheeks flair pink, proving I can make her blush. I

squeeze her hand and lead her to an empty bench. "What else do you want to do?"

"You keep letting me choose. It's making me anxious. What do you want to do?" she insists.

"I'm with you doing something I've wanted to do for years. That's more than enough ... but we are ending with the Ferris wheel," I point out.

"Then it sounds like we should go on the slingshot," she says as she points at a ride.

A second later, people connected to Bungie cords or something are shot into the air and left to drop, bounce, and just fall. My stomach falls into my ass just watching them. I take a slow breath. "You trust that?"

"More than I trust you leaving for work and coming back in one piece."

She'd been frustrated when I refused to go to the hospital again and came to her bleeding enough to need to use her hair straightener. I did replace it with the best model that Stephanie recommended.

"If it's a no, that's fine. I'm not your brothers. I will not make you feel bad," Abby assures me. "No, is okay."

I meet her eyes, still blown away by how sweet she is. She could ruin me with my brothers–saying I'm afraid of spiders, clowns, and stupid rides that are almost always fine. Still, I trust her not to. Abby has never made me feel less than when I tell her how I'm feeling, what I'm afraid of, what I enjoy.

Hell, I was so proud I made cookies from scratch for her that Ed gave me shit for sounding 'smiley' when he called me over the phone. Abby's not like that, though. She's warm and accepting. Her teasing is always gentle, makes me feel seen rather than humiliated.

"Let's go," I decide.

"What? No, Danya, you don't have to do this for me. It's not fun unless we both enjoy it."

"Let's start with the coaster then," I suggest.

We do just that. Abby holds onto me and screams along with everyone else. I smile at her and enjoy the ride. It's a nice adrenaline high that I'm going to use to get on the stupid "slingshot". When we get in line, she bounces.

"I'm excited about this. I've seen plenty around, you know. I tried to get my parents to go with me, friends in high school, but everyone called me crazy and said I should go alone," she admits. "It's one of those rides I don't want to do with a stranger."

"First time together," I say.

She blinks a few times. "Huh."

"What?"

"Is this the first time we're both doing something we haven't done before? I've shared plenty of the things I like with you and you've done that with me, but..."

I kiss her and cup the back of her neck in my hand, not caring that whoever's behind us is clearing their throat since we're not moving forward right away. When I draw back, I tug Abby forward.

Eventually we're strapped into the ride and I grip Abby's hand so tightly, I'm worried I'm going to break her. She doesn't shake me off, doesn't tell me to stop, she just holds on, squeezing my hand while taking a deep breath.

"It'll be even more of a rush than the coaster," she promises.

Before I can answer, we're shot into the air. I let out a yell as Abby does the same. I turn to watch her, unwilling to stare at the sky or the ground, just wanting to see her. Her smile is far too big, her eyes squinted as she yells and laughs.

In less than a minute, the ride is over, but I'm still staring at her. Her flushed face, her gorgeous blonde hair a mess, her brown eyes on me, reflecting the stars or the lights of the rides or whatever they're catching.

I *love* her. How can I not?

She's fierce, handles everything in my life with a kind of grace that I can't fathom, all while still being warm and sweet until she has to be something else. We have plenty to take on in our relationship—her meeting my father; me meeting her parents—and more to figure out, but right now, in this exact moment, it takes every bit of control to keep the words from falling out of my mouth.

"And on to the Ferris wheel?" she guesses as we escape the restraints of the ride.

"We're going to be doing a lot more than looking at the scenery," I warn her with a smile, not sure how else to process what I'm feeling.

"I figured that, since we're going to be alone," she says with a wink, dragging me toward the last ride like an eager little kid.

TWENTY

Abby

STARING OUT OVER THE PIER AND ACROSS THE OCEAN, noticing how the lights catch on the crest of waves, I sigh against Danya. He turns my chin to face him. "Top of the Ferris wheel, Cupcake."

The car is nice and spacious, with glass windows all around until I feel like we're in a safe little ball. It also has the benefit of no seatbelts. I smile at Danya until his lips come down on mine. He strokes my side, his fingers brushing the sides of my breast before he teases the tie of my shirt. A loud moan leaves my throat as he shoves his hand into my shirt.

"You didn't wear a bra?" He growls against my lips.

"Shame you can't find out what else I didn't wear," I answer with a smile.

He groans and pulls me tighter against him, pinching and tugging my nipple as we continue to make out. I've started trying new things to excite him and myself. Danya makes me feel sexy all the time, so desired, so beautiful that I don't second guess it when I decide not to wear underwear or when I decide to wear something a little on the sultry side, like my shirt today.

Danya pulls the tie on my shirt, then spreads my shirt as his mouth slides down my throat. He pushes me back to suck my nipple between his lips as his other hand slides to my shorts. He undoes the button, the zipper, then my breath catches in my throat.

"Here?" I ask in a squeak.

His other hand grips my hair, jerking me back so I'm almost entirely exposed to him. He jerks my shorts down further. "You're practically naked, *Zhizn moya*. How am I supposed to resist?"

"Well ... you're not," I admit.

He grins and kisses me again, deeply his fingers pushing deeper into my shorts until he brushes my clit and I moan against his lips. He smiles instead of kissing me again. "Like I said, you need to buy some skirts. I could have you on my lap," his finger pushes into my pussy, making me whimper. "Could be buried inside you while licking and sucking your nipples." He works another finger into me and struggles to finger me the way he wants to, considering how restricted his hand is. "Coming apart on our second go around."

"Danya!" I try to hide my face, but his hand in my hair can't be argued with.

He shakes his head. "You don't get to hide from me. But you better come fast. I'm not moving my hand from right here until you do and those ride operators might get distracted seeing you on the edge."

I adjust my hips so he can get deeper and he groans, lowering his mouth to my nipple again. He bites at my breast, flattens his tongue over my nipple, drives me insane until I can barely think.

"So wet for me, Abby."

"Yes," I pant.

"I bet you wish you had my cock right here," he curls his fingers against my g-spot to prove his point, "filling your sweet pussy."

"Your fingers feel so good," I try to argue.

"As good as my tongue?" he sucks my nipple between his lips and flicks his tongue over the sensitive bud while fucking me faster with his fingers.

The combination breaks me in record time. I come apart, whimpering, and squirming, trying to hold back so that way I don't soak my shorts. Danya eases up and hums against my skin. He captures me in a passionate, insatiable kiss, then frees his fingers from my shorts.

Before he can slide his fingers into his mouth, I grab his wrist and suck them clean myself. It always riles him. He hates when I steal what he wants. He growls and pushes me down onto the rather uncomfortable bench to kiss me, his tongue teasing mine before he sucks it, determined to taste me.

Somehow—I'm not sure how—but we end up dressed and proper for the public by the time we get off. Danya still has a hard on that his jeans aren't hiding. More than a few women check him out.

"You, sit right here. I'll get us some fried chicken and a funnel cake," he decides. "Soda?"

"Coke," I answer with a smile. "Thank you!"

As he goes to stand in line, I see women fawning over him. Plenty are trying to talk to him, but he turns his distant gaze on them. Danya is many things. I know that just from these last few weeks together, but when it comes to flirting, he shuts it down faster than anyone I know. He flirts only when it serves a purpose, unless it's with me.

When one woman pushes her luck by touching him, he just arches an eyebrow at her, saying nothing, just staring. Eventually it gets to her. She blushes, pulls her hand away and skitters back with her friends.

I almost can't believe there was a time where I *told him* to have fun with other women as long as my ex and I didn't see. I rest my elbow on the table and put my cheek in my hand as I watch him.

He's gorgeous. His blond hair picks up the neon lights, his blue eyes are piercing, even with this distance between us. I blink, watching him as my phone buzzes. Danya licks his bottom lip, reminding me of what we were doing in the Ferris Wheel and why the tie on my shirt is so messy.

I look down at my phone.

Danya: Enjoying the view?

I glance back at him, and he winks at me while raising the receipt. I giggle and glance around. Before I can get up to join him, someone blocks my path. I blink a few times and find Aaron there. Aaron, who should have given up weeks ago.

"Aw, are you all alone now, 'cupcake'?" he asks mockingly.

"No."

"Seems like it. Wish I could give you a pity date, but I've moved on," he says, a woman with flaming red hair on his arm. She looks bored as she checks out her nails.

"Cool, have fun," I advise him.

He shakes his head. "It's pitiful that you're still fake dating a guy just to make yourself feel better."

Rolling my eyes feels like an excellent answer, but a second later, he's shoved out of the way as Lilah and Stephanie join me. I jump up, looking between them. "What are you guys doing here?"

"Edmon checked Danya's location and couldn't believe it," Lilah giggles.

"And Aleks is at some kind of wedding thing–I think meeting Sienna's parents? I don't know. It was tense, and I figured they didn't need to meet me." Stephanie waves her hand.

"Oh, you're not step mommy yet?" Lilah teases.

"You say that like you *want* me to ground Ed," Stephanie laughs.

It took a while for Stephanie and Lilah to tell me that Stephanie and Ed were seeing each other before Ed got with Lilah and now Stephanie is dating the brothers' father. It's kind of messy, but they make it work with an ease that has me jealous.

"Where's Danya?" Edmon asks, wrapping his arm around Lilah's hip.

"Don't say that like you don't want to be around me," Stephanie teases.

"Behave children," Lilah orders. "I had to break up four fights this week. I don't want to break up another one."

Ed groans and buries his face in her hair. He says something that makes her eyes widen and he gives her a wicked smile. Stephanie rolls her eyes as they run off somewhere. Steph shakes her head. "Lilah and I started going to kick boxing class and now she elbows the gym teacher out of the way to break up fights between kids taller than her. Ed loves it."

"Foreplay?" I guess.

Stephanie laughs. "I like you. You don't beat around the bush."

"Sometimes I do," I admit. "Are you going to be Aleks' date at the wedding next week?"

"Of course! His ex wife will be there though and I'm worried it will be a mess, but ... I love him and want to be there with him. It's that simple," Stephanie answers. "Are you going?"

I laugh. "I'm bringing the cake. Of course I'm going. I'll be at the reception, making sure that-"

"Abby, that's not what I mean," Stephanie says. She looks over and groans. "Okay, I have to go make sure Ed doesn't get my best friend thrown in jail for indecent exposure. Horny honeymoon phase needs to wear off."

She hurries away, yelling Ed's name and ordering him not to run from "step-mommy."

Danya comes back and shakes his head. "You'll never be bored in my family."

"I'm never bored with you," I counter.

We eat and talk about the carnival, about games we haven't played and want to play. He's sure he can beat me in darts and a shooting game. We go through it all and I give *him* a purple panda when I kick his butt in darts.

After that, we just walk, hand in hand, along the pier to look out over the ocean. Danya clears his throat. "What were you talking about with Stephanie and Lilah?"

"Your twin couldn't believe you were here," I report, "so he came to see for himself."

Danya rolls his eyes.

"And the wedding. Sienna and Lev are having dinner with parents and ... I can't believe the wedding is next weekend."

"Are you ready?" he asks. "With the cake? I know the mascarpone has been giving you trouble."

"I just can't get it to be as light as I want it. I've tried using different sugars, whipping it a bit more. I mean, it's supposed to be kind of dense so it seeps into the cake itself, but it still seems a bit too heavy with the strawberries too. Everything else has been easy. I did sugar sculpting to make the pearls and decorations and-"

"Will you go to the wedding with me?" Danya asks.

He doesn't normally cut me off after asking me a question. I face him and cock my head to the side. "You know I'm going to be there."

"And you don't have to guard the cake all night. Come to the ceremony with me and be with me at the reception ... as my girlfriend," he asks, almost shyly.

I take a step towards him. "You want to take that step in front of people from your world?"

"I'm going to have to eat my pride in a few conversations, but yes. I want to be your boyfriend, Abby. I want to do it the right way, the normal way."

"Are you ... sure?"

"I kind of asked you to move in earlier today. Asking you to be my date to the wedding should be less surprising," he says with a forced laugh. He looks over the ocean and rubs the back of his neck. "I didn't want any kind of relationship ever. I thought my brothers were weak and distracted and losing touch with who we are. We *are* the mafia, but ..."

"But?"

"But you make me want to be more than that," he admits, tugging me against him. "Even if we need to work on your aim with a gun and your willingness to treat people you don't know a little too kindly."

I look up at him, the hopeful, boyish smile on his face. I stand on my toes and kiss him, nibbling his bottom lip. "Of course I'll be your date to the wedding, Danya."

"No hesitations?"

"None. After all, now I have to be your fake girlfriend," I tease with a shrug.

He curses in Russian and opens his mouth to yell at me, but I pull him close again and grin. "Before you say no, I'm very thorough and dedicated to the ruse. I might even get confused into thinking we're together."

"No more fake, Abigail. Everything's real," he growls against my lips.

TWENTY-ONE

Epilogue: Danya

1 WEEK LATER

"Where is the cake?!" Lev asks when he sees me. "It's late. We wanted it here before the wedding to make sure everything was set. We have pictures to take, we have final touches to do and-"

I cross my arms over my chest. He huffs. "I'll call her. I want to see it right here and-"

"The cake is already here. It's in the fridge, staying chilled so that way it keeps through the reception. My girlfriend isn't going to let something fall through the cracks," I growl defensively.

Lev struggles with his tie for the fifth time, his fingers just not cooperating. I do it for him, then turn him over to Edmon so he can take care of our brother. I've never seen him this nervous. I text Abby, then slip out of the room and find her there, wearing a gorgeous pale pink dress that isn't *too* sexy, but is too expensive for me to tear off her.

It's a shame. I'm all too happy to break flimsy zippers and hear the scream of seams as I pull clothes off her. I run my hands through my hair thinking about it, but she puts her hand on my chest, like she can read my mind. "No, you behave. You can't have lipstick on you when you're up at the altar. Be good."

I take a frustrated breath. "Lev got worried about the cake, but I took care of it. It looks amazing."

"Thanks. I hope the bride and groom agree." Her teeth press into her lower lip and her lipstick doesn't move. I narrow my eyes and she jumps up, pointing at me. "No. If we start, we won't stop. I should have worn regular lipstick because then-"

I jerk her against me and kiss her. I deepen the kiss, losing myself in the slow burn of desire that courses between us. Abby resists for all of ten seconds before she's melting against me. I wrap my arm around her waist and grab her ass since I have a feeling her hair is off-limits.

She moans into my mouth until I release her. She fans herself. "You're not allowed to do that, Danya."

"Not until after they cut the cake and we can ditch this popsicle stand?" I ask while wiggling my eyebrows.

She huffs. "I shouldn't have taught you that phrase."

"It's as cute as you are. Now, I have to go calm my brother down, so he gets down the fucking aisle. After that, I'm all yours. Use me ruthlessly."

"Well ... when you say it like that, how can I refuse?" She asks with a soft giggle before kissing my neck. "I'll only be looking at you through the wedding."

That thought stays with me and distracts me throughout the ceremony. I know that Sienna is crying and plenty of people in the crowd are tearing up, but when I see Abby watching me, her eyes watering as she gives me a soft smile that spells out how I've been feeling for her the last week, my heart lodges in my throat.

Even though I traded all our tickets in for that mood ring when we were at the pier, I haven't given it to her. Giving her a ring that's not an engagement ring doesn't feel right. But giving her a promise ring might work out better. I know it's old-fashioned and something I'm pretty sure teenagers do. I want her to know how serious I am about her and how much she's changed me.

"Pay attention," Abby mouths, making me laugh as I look over at my brother and Sienna as they kiss. Sienna hops into Lev's arms and the kiss they share is not fit for the public.

Lev grips her hair, ruining it as he devours her. She grips his jacket right at the buttons, pulling him against her like it's the first and only kiss, like their entire relationship has built up to this moment and not giving it everything would be a disservice.

When they break apart, people cheer and they run off. I know we have to take pictures, but I have a feeling they're going to be busy for at least ten minutes. Everyone else files out as my father goes to get the happy couple.

I remind myself pictures are important, and we have to look happy. Between shots, I see blatant frustration on Lev's face. He wants Sienna, and he wants her *now*. After a few more, I clear my throat. "I think there are plenty of the bride and groom. They have a long night of partying ahead and probably need a second to catch their breath."

The photographer nods, but catches us before we can follow Sienna and Lev out of the venue. We take pictures as the wedding party, then get to go to the reception hall. I look around and am stopped by the Volkov brothers, Lief and Valerie. They're standing between me and my goal.

Lief wraps himself around their wife.

"There's music playing. Would you like to dance?" I catch him say as I approach.

Chase motions for them to do just that as Hunter raises a glass, enjoying the view of his wife walking away. He sees me and pats my chest. "The only bachelor left in the family!"

"About that ..."

Chase smirks. "Someone catch you?"

"I'm sure you two cursed me," I point at them in accusation. "I was fine, not falling for anyone, and then you two started talking."

"We're not paying for the wedding," Hunter decides.

I shake my head. "Please, Ed should get on that first. He and Lilah have been together much longer."

"As if that matters," Chase laughs. "Who's the girl?"

"I'm looking for her. She's my date, but she's working too," I answer.

"Are you going to tell us the whole story? If so, we should make sure Valerie can't hear us. We want all the details," Hunter says with a wink.

I narrow my eyes at him. "I don't want to be on your wife's hit list."

Spotting Abby over his shoulder double and triple checking the cake. I know she's going to drive herself crazy if I don't distract her. I pat Hunter's shoulder. "Another night, when I know she won't overhear."

"Well," Chase hesitates.

"As if either of you will focus if she's out here dancing and mingling without you," I hint.

They both look over as she dances with Lief, not slow dancing. Hunter groans. "She does that in public and just assumes no one will try to get on her other side."

They rush off and I wander over to Abby. I stroke through her hair, then pull her against me. She huffs. "Taken. Off."

"Are you taken? I thought you were a thorough and diligent girlfriend," I purr in her ear.

She turns around; her face flaring red. "Danya!"

"Cupcake," I greet. "The cake is perfect. Walk away."

"But what if-"

"If you keep worrying about it, no one is going to eat it. You did a great job."

"But the mascarpone might fail and if it does, I'll have to remake the cake and then it will be a mess," she argues.

"I tasted the mascarpone—it's perfect. We tested it in mini-cakes. You remembered the supports. You're a professional and you've done your job well," I say, trying to convince her.

She looks at the cake with me and takes a few breaths. "You're right. I'm just finding things to worry about."

"You should worry about me. If you're not here to distract me, I might do something wild, like running away with the baker," I warn her.

She laughs and gets onto the dance floor with me before sitting beside me at the table. She holds my hand under the table. "I'm happy to be here with you, Danya. As your girlfriend and.."

"And?"

"And I would like to move in with you … if the offer is still available. I think we'll be ready for it in another three weeks," she answers, while playing with her hair.

I pull her towards me and kiss her deeply showing her how much that little comment means to me. I groan when I hear cheers, since that means that Sienna and Lev are back and things are happening.

"I want you out of here already. There are plenty of closets, stairwells, private areas," I groan.

"Soon we won't have to find places," Abby teases.

I lean toward her. "I know there's a kitchen here."

"With people in it," she giggles.

"You're driving me insane," I say, sighing.

"Let's wait until some things are going on. Then we can sneak away without worrying about you getting into trouble," she hints before touching my thigh, "for the wrong thing."

I take a slow breath because I have to resist her for now. I manage thirty minutes of waiting before I take her hand, acting like I'm going to drag her to the dance floor, but end up pulling her away and up a set of service stairs. When we get to the first landing, I press Abby against a wall and I kiss her with a deliberate slowness, creating a moment suspended in time. It's so easy to lose myself in her.

When she makes a little whimpering, moaning sound, I remember the smile she gave me during the ceremony. I draw back and she kisses my chest after undoing a few buttons. "We don't have long, Danya. We need to-"

"I love you," I say.

She blinks a few times as she draws back, staring up at me. She rubs her ear. "W-what?"

"I *love* you, *Zhizn moya*," I answer. "You asked me what that means once."

She blushes and rubs my chest without meeting my eyes. "I looked it up. I know what it means, Danya."

"Then me loving you shouldn't be a surprise. You make me feel alive," I whisper, trying to pull her closer against me. "You're my life, Cupcake."

She takes a ragged breath. "Those words mean a lot."

"I'm well aware. I didn't think I'd say them in this lifetime," I admit.

"*Sakharok* ... I love you too," she murmurs, her cheeks burning.

I stare at her. "What did you call me?"

"Did I say it right? I practiced. It's supposed to mean 'sugar' or something and I thought it fit because you call me cupcake and-"

I kiss her, licking deep into her mouth and only pry away when I feel myself hard. "Again. Say it again."

"*Sakharok*," she pants.

I kiss her again and again. I deepen the kiss, letting the intensity of the moment blossom between us, then pry myself away when she rubs against me, eager and willing, although anyone could walk in. I reach into my pocket and show her the mood ring. I hold it up.

"Danya?"

"I got this at the pier with the tickets from our winnings ... it's a promise for our future. Nothing but a promise," I say, assuring her. "I will not move too fast with you. But I want you to know that I'm not going anywhere. You will not lose me by being you."

She stares at the ring and puts it on her thumb—it's the only finger it fits. It turns light green after a moment and I pull out the little slip of paper that comes with it. Light green means romantic.

"So?" I ask.

"I love it, and I love you, Danya. All of you, every bit of you," she says before jerking me down and kissing me with an intensity, savoring the depth of our connection.

Her sweetness doesn't taste like anything but pure joy now.

9 798215 613740